Treachery at the River Canyon

CROSSWAY BOOKS BY STEPHEN BLY

THE STUART BRANNON WESTERN SERIES

Hard Winter at Broken Arrow Crossing
False Claims at the Little Stephen Mine
Last Hanging at Paradise Meadow
Standoff at Sunrise Creek
Final Justice at Adobe Wells
Son of an Arizona Legend

THE NATHAN T. RIGGINS WESTERN
ADVENTURE SERIES
(Ages 9–14)

The Dog Who Would Not Smile
Coyote True
You Can Always Trust a Spotted Horse
The Last Stubborn Buffalo in Nevada
Never Dance with a Bobcat
Hawks Don't Say Goodbye

THE CODE OF THE WEST SERIES

It's Your Misfortune & None of My Own
One Went to Denver & the Other Went Wrong
Where the Deer & the Antelope Play
Stay Away From That City . . . They Call It Cheyenne
My Foot's in the Stirrup . . . My Pony Won't Stand

THE AUSTIN-STONER FILES

The Lost Manuscript of Martin Taylor Harrison
The Final Chapter of Chance McCall

THE LEWIS AND CLARK SQUAD ADVENTURE SERIES
(Ages 9–14)

Intrigue at the Rafter B Ranch
The Secret of the Old Rifle
Treachery at the River Canyon

LEWIS and CLARK
SQUAD
BOOK THREE

Treachery at the River Canyon

S T E P H E N   B L Y

CROSSWAY BOOKS • WHEATON, ILLINOIS
A DIVISION OF GOOD NEWS PUBLISHERS

BLY

Treachery at the River Canyon

Published by Crossway Books
a division of Good News Publishers
1300 Crescent Street
Wheaton, Illinois 60187

Cover illustration: Sergio Giovine

Cover design: Cindy Kiple

First printing, 1997

Printed in the United States of America

Library of Congress Cataloging-in-Publication Data
Bly, Stephen, 1944-
   Treachery at the River Canyon / Stephen Bly.
     p.   cm.—(The Lewis & Clark Squad adventure series ; bk. 3)
   Summary: Having become involved in theft among nighttime river rafters and rivalry between two teams, the Lewis and Clark Squad learns to trust in God even more than before.
   ISBN 0-89107-941-6
   [1. Gangs—Fiction. 2. Rafting (Sports)—Fiction. 3. Christian life—Fiction.] II. Series: Bly, Stephen A., 1944-   Lewis & Clark Squad adventure series ; bk. 3
PZ7.B6275Tp 1997
[Fic]—dc21   96-40088

05		04		03		02		01		00		99		98		97
15	14	13	12	11	10	9	8	7	6	5	4	3	2	1

For my good pal
Cole Riggers

cording

e called
st places
a logging
n moun-
nd skid-
own hair
his bare

ther home.

. Levine,"
week like

he said he would.

him he needs to p

Ride my bicyc

only eight miles d

uphill to go home.

Good, old Cod

The temperatu

Idaho rose drama

River Canyon. Th

trees. Nothing bu

rocks could be see

And Cody cou

A hundred mil

Across the rive

ited Joseph Plains

Devils Mountains

America's deepest

Lord, this is like

down it you go, the f

you end up. I alway

prospectors panning

Nez Perce hunting el

The column of th

Cody to mumble ou

like a mad man, an

river! I don't need th

As the dust roa

canyon, Cody notice

pickup.

That's Mr. Levine

One

❖

A good day for Cody Clark was one that went according to plan.

His plan.

This was not a good day.

He coasted down the gravel and dirt lane called Cemetery Creek Road. It was wide enough in most places to allow two rigs to pass, provided one was not a logging truck. The knobby tires on his steel-gray and green mountain bike bounced and scooted as they banged and skidded from rock to dusty rock. His shaggy dark brown hair flagged in the breeze, which felt faintly cool on his bare arms and lower legs.

Denver and Dad are at the ranch.

Townie went with his grandpa to bring his mother home.

Mom's working at the post office.

Feather's still sleeping.

And me?

"I want you to ride down and check on Mr. Levine," Mom had said. "He didn't come into town this week like he said he would. He has a registered letter to sign for. Tell him he needs to pick it up by Friday."

Ride my bicycle out to Mr. Levine's? Oh, sure, Mom. It's only eight miles downhill to get there. And a zillion miles uphill to go home.

Good, old Cody. He'll do it. Cody, the slave.

The temperature of the early July day in north-central Idaho rose dramatically as he descended into the Salmon River Canyon. The mountainside soon became barren of trees. Nothing but dry brown grass and jagged granite rocks could be seen for miles.

And Cody could see for miles.

A hundred miles.

Across the river stretched the high, almost uninhabited Joseph Plains. Beyond them, the peaks of the Seven Devils Mountains, sentinels of Hell's Canyon—North America's deepest gorge.

Lord, this is like a road back into history. The farther down it you go, the farther away from the twentieth century you end up. I always feel that if I'd just keep going, I'd find prospectors panning for gold, Chief Joseph and his Wallowa Nez Perce hunting elk, or old Jim Bridger trapping beaver.

The column of thick, red dust headed his way caused Cody to mumble out loud, "Oh, great. Someone's driving like a mad man, and I'll be eating dust all the way to the river! I don't need this."

As the dust roared up the road leading out of the canyon, Cody noticed that it came from a 1952 faded black pickup.

That's Mr. Levine's outfit! He's probably going to town

right now. *If Mom hadn't been in such a hurry, I could have stayed home! I'll flag him down. Maybe he'll give me a ride back to town.*

As the pickup roared up the road, Cody heard the grinding of gears. The truck backfired. Then its rear end fishtailed in the gravel, which caused even more dust to billow into the air.

I didn't know Mr. Levine drove so fast! I sure hope he doesn't meet a logging truck or something.

I hope he slows down a little!

Cody coasted over to the left side of the road and dismounted from his bike. He watched the old pickup rattle and bounce its way toward him.

He's going too fast—way too fast! I don't think he even sees me.

"Hey! Mr. Levine, it's me—Cody! I need to talk to you!" Holding the handlebars of his bike with his left hand, he waved at the oncoming truck with his right.

He's coming right at me! What's he doing? Lord, this isn't a very funny joke! Slow down! He's trying to . . .

Cody shoved his bicycle to the road and dove into the grass and rock culvert that separated the road from the cliff. He felt the palms of his hands rub raw as they skidded into the granite chips. His left leg slammed into a half-buried boulder, and he rolled toward the edge of the cliff as he struggled to sit up.

That's not . . .

The pickup seemed to swerve purposely to the right and clip the front tire on Cody's bike.

"Hey!" he yelled from his sitting position.

The cloud of dust hung in the air. Cody could hear the roar of the engine, but he could no longer see the pickup.

"That wasn't Mr Levine! There were two guys in that truck. And they tried to run me down!"

He searched for a clean spot on his sleeveless black ProRodeo T-shirt to wipe his eyes.

"What's going on? What is this?" Gingerly brushing the dirt and dust off his legs and jeans shorts, he looked again at his scratched red hands and then at his broken bike.

They tried to kill me, Lord.

At least, they tried to scare me.

Well, it worked.

That bike cost me $269 plus tax. Look at it. The front tire busted, wheel mangled, fork bent, hand brake dangling. I—I . . .

Cody fought to hold back the tears.

I'm not going to cry. I'm thirteen years old. Five feet, seven inches—134 pounds. I am not a kid. I'm tough enough to buck hay, break horses, and face down J. J. Melton. I'm certainly too tough to cry.

He could feel the tears streaming down his dirt-caked cheeks.

Yeah, right!

Lord, what do I do now? Walk home? Walk on down to Mr. Levine's? Mom said if I wasn't home when she went for lunch, she'd drive down and give me a ride. Cody glanced up at the position of the sun. *But that's a couple hours from now.*

He picked up the bent and broken bike and, balancing it on the back wheel, began to roll it on down the gravel road. He could feel the salt from the sweat on his hand burn into the cuts in his palms.

Lord, it seems like You sort of missed it on this one. Why did this have to happen to me? If it hadn't been for my quick reaction, I would have gotten run over.

Of course, I guess You did have something to do with that, didn't You?

The point is, this day sure could have been a whole lot better!

When Cody reached the slowly decaying hulk of the land-locked stern-wheeler, *The Pride of Astoria*, his arms throbbed from balancing the bicycle on one tire. He abandoned the mountain bike against the bulkhead of the ancient steamboat and slowly hiked up Chad Levine's long inclining driveway.

Maybe he sold his truck. No, he wouldn't sell his only vehicle. Maybe he bought a new one. He sure has enough cash filed in that shoe box. But if he hasn't bought one after all these years, why do it now?

Of course, it could be just a coincidence. Maybe those guys were just driving through the area in an identical rig.

Not likely, Clark.

Chad Levine's big log cabin sat on a knoll about 200 feet above the Salmon River. To the north stretched steep, gently rolling, grass-covered mountains. His big bay window and porch faced south where he could survey the river, canyon, and mountains. Cody figured it was the best view in the state of Idaho. Maybe even in the whole world!

Stepping to the back screen door, Cody hollered, "Mr. Levine? Are you there, Mr. Levine?"

Maybe he's at the barn. I sure hope he didn't take the sheep out on the hills for the day.

Cody hiked to the barn and continued to call out. A horse, a mule, and a donkey were crowded into the one shady spot in the pasture, trying to sleep and swat flies with their tails.

"Mr. Levine? It's me—Cody Clark."

The barn . . . the tool shed . . . the blacksmith shop . . . the outhouse . . . were all unoccupied.

His pickup is gone. But I'm sure he wasn't in it. If he's out in the canyon, they could have stolen it without him knowing it.

Cody finally plodded to the front porch of the one-room cabin. The floor-to-ceiling windows reflected the panorama of the canyon like a large mirror. In the midst of the picture Cody spotted a thirteen-year-old kid with dirty, tear-streaked face, red and raw hands, and uncombed hair. The kid wore Wranglers cut off at the knees, a black sleeveless T-shirt that would have read "Rodeo Attitude: It Ain't Fer City Boys" if it hadn't been plastered with dirt, and black high-top tennis shoes with dusty white socks sagging.

"Cody Clark," he addressed the image in the window, "you are a mess! You look like you got hung up in the stirrup and drug a mile across the prairie. Clean yourself up and leave Mr. Levine a note."

He knocked at the front door and then shoved it open about three inches. "Mr. Levine? It's me—Cody Clark."

After an extremely long ten seconds of silence, Cody pushed the door all the way open.

I don't think he'd mind if I used a little of that spring water to wash up.

He stepped over the threshold and into the large wood-paneled multipurpose room. The room was a little dark, and while as cluttered as ever, Cody was struck by its neatness. Every pile of old newspapers, every magazine, every book was stacked carefully in its place.

Cody wasn't sure which caught his eye first—the discarded empty shoe box that he had seen only a week earlier stuffed with $100 bills or the worn packer boots of Chad Levine sticking out from behind the brown leather sofa. Holding his breath, he cautiously spied around the couch. The sight caused his temples to tighten and his stomach to drop.

"Mr. Levine!" he choked, trying to suck in air as he spoke.

The old shepherd lay on his stomach on the worn wooden floor of the huge cabin. His head was straight down on the wood, hiding his gray-bearded face from Cody's view.

Oh, man . . . it was those guys. They stole his money, took his truck . . .

What if he's dead?

No, no . . . I don't . . .

Cody's arms began to shake uncontrollably. He rocked back and forth on his feet.

I don't know what to do, Lord! I didn't want to come down here. My mother made me. She ought to be here. What if he's dead? What if they come back to make sure? What if they saw me turn in here and come to eliminate me, too? I've got to do something.

I've got to hide.

I'll run up into the mountains.

Maybe I should go down to the river.

I wish Dad were here.

Or Mom.

Or Denver.

Anybody but me!

"Mr. Levine? Are you all right?"

Cody dropped to his hands and knees and stared at the old man lying on the floor. He thought he could see a little dried blood in the thick, matted gray hair at the back of his head.

"Don't move an injured person, or you might injure him more," he muttered. "What if he's dead?"

Is he breathing? Lord, You've got to help Mr. Levine . . . eh, I think maybe You better help me, too!

Take his pulse . . . I mean, find out if he has a pulse. On television they put their hand on a guy's neck. But where on the neck?

With a trembling hand, Cody reached out to the old man's wrinkled and leathery tough neck. He felt the rough stubble of his beard.

Where is it? I can't find it. He is dead! Oh, man . . . no!

Cody felt a little dizzy. His vision blurred. He seemed to be looking down a long tunnel.

Come on, Clark. You're not going to pass out.

Cody sat on the floor of the cabin and pulled his knees

up in front of him. Then he held his hands on the sides of his face and dropped his head to his knees. He closed his eyes and began to take big, deep breaths.

Stay alert, Cody Wayne Clark. Let your mind clear. Get some oxygen in your lungs. Don't panic!

Man, if I don't get to panic now, when do I?

When he opened his eyes, the room was no longer spinning in front of him. With his hands still clutching his head, he avoided looking at Mr. Levine's body and gazed out the window.

He took another big, deep breath and sighed. "Well, at least I'm not going to do something dumb like passing out!"

His mind began to clear, his vision relaxed to normal, and he could feel his heart beat fast as his hands clutched his face.

"Heartbeat! That's where you find it!" His thumbs pushed into his neck right under his jawbone. Cody looked down at Chad Levine.

"Okay. You can do it. No big deal. Just reach right over and . . ."

For a moment, Cody felt as if he were looking down on the scene from above, and it was some other boy who reached back over to the old man's neck. With three fingers pressed against the neck, he held his breath.

"There it is!" he shouted. "All right! It's beating, Lord. It really is. He's alive!"

What do I do now?

How long will he be alive?

He needs help—an ambulance.

No telephone. No fax. No E-mail. No cellular. No CB. No neighbors. No nothing!

Cemetery Creek Road! Maybe I can go flag someone down. If anyone's out there. Someone has to come along. Lord, You've got to send someone. Please!

"Mr. Levine, I'm going to go and try to find some help. I'm not moving you, because I'm afraid to make things worse. So just, eh, stay right there until I get back."

Cody sprinted out the front door, off the porch, and across the packed-dirt yard. The air, even though fairly warm, felt cool on his sweat-covered face and arms. Chad Levine's mile-long dirt driveway sloped steeply down to Cemetery Creek Road. Cody found a steady pace but could feel a slight pain in his left side where he had hit the rock when he dove off the roadway to avoid the pickup. A column of dust swirled down the road, headed south toward the Salmon River. Cody knew that under that dust was a vehicle of some sort.

"I've got to get to the road before he passes by!" he mumbled, lengthening his stride.

The bluff next to the road kept Cody from seeing the vehicle itself, but he could watch the column of dust approach the intersection with Levine's driveway.

He's going too fast. I'll never get there in time.

Cody almost stumbled out of control as he hurled himself down the drive.

Slow down, Clark, or you'll crash! Never run downhill. But I've got to make it, Lord! I've just got to. Have them slow down. Have them look up this driveway!

Glancing through the wrecked hull of *The Pride of*

Astoria, Cody spotted the source of the dust column—a white Jeep with a black ragtop. But in staring at the Jeep, he lost sight of the driveway, twisting his right ankle. Thoughts of crashing headlong into the gravel caused him to launch himself into the tall, dry weeds behind the old steamboat.

"Lord, stop the Jeep!"

The ground beneath the weeds was sandy and rock-free. Cody had a fairly soft landing. He rolled to his knees and waved his arms.

"Hey! Stop! Wait! I need help!" he screamed.

They went on! Lord, I need a break. Why didn't You stop that guy?

Cody rolled over on his back and caught his breath, then stood, and brushed himself off. His knees were now about as raw as his hands. He inched his way out to the road and squinted down toward the Salmon River.

He's headed down to fish. Maybe I should go down there and try to find him.

Cody hiked back to the hull of the steamship and sat down on the decaying wood next to his mangled bicycle.

Someone else has to come along. At least Mom will be here in an hour or so. Let's see, in an hour I can hike three to four miles—but it's uphill. The Buckhorn Ranch is five miles up the grade. But they passed me with a truck load of hay headed toward town.

Someone will be along soon.

Cody looked down at his dirt-covered shorts and legs.

"You've got to get cleaned up, Clark. Someone's bound to come by. 'Course, I don't know who," he muttered.

"Maybe those guys in Mr. Levine's pickup will be back. Isn't there something about returning to the scene of the crime? I can't just sit out here like a yearling in a bog hole!"

Jumping down from his perch on the steamboat, Cody trudged up the driveway. *This is crazy. It's like everything I do today is the wrong thing. Every moment it gets more complicated than the last one.*

Cody's mouth was so dry the dust tasted bitter as it fogged up around him. He jogged across the yard. Both legs now hurt when he ran. He banged his way through the screen door.

"Mr. Levine? Did you come to yet?"

The old shepherd still lay in the exact same silent position.

"Lord, something's got to happen. This can't just go on like this." He walked over to the sink in the center of the wall-length counter.

The water pressure was light, but the stream was ice cold. He pulled off his sleeveless T-shirt and leaned over the sink. He caught a big double handful of water and splashed it on his face.

"Ahhh!" he hollered, trying to catch his breath.

Over and over he splashed on the water until his face, neck, and arms felt clean. Then he turned off the water and searched for a towel.

Man, that water's so cold it would raise the dead! . . . Mr. Levine!

Cody filled a clean coffee cup full of water and scurried over to Chad Levine.

I can't believe I didn't think of this earlier. It always works in the movies!

Cody heard a vehicle pull up in the yard.

"They're coming back!" he gasped. He hurriedly tossed the water at Mr. Levine's head. Most of it landed on the man's neck and splashed against the side of his face. Cody ran to the back and peeked out the screen door.

"Mom!"

"Young Mr. Clark!" a weak and raspy voice called to him from behind the sofa. "Did you pour this water on me?"

Cody spun around. Chad Levine was propped up on one hand.

"Mr. Levine, you're alive! I mean, you came to!" Cody cried out. "Wow, that's great!"

"With an extremely painful bump on the back of my head!" he moaned and reached out for the arm of the sofa in an attempt to pull himself up. "Can you help me to my feet?"

Cody started back toward the sofa.

"Cody Wayne? Are you in there?"

His mother's voice boomed through the screen on the back door.

"Mom, in here. Hurry. Mr. Levine's been hurt!" he hollered.

Margaret Clark rushed in.

"Cody, where's your shirt? Are you all right?" She wrapped her tanned, strong arm around his shoulder.

"Yeah." He felt as if a 100-pound rock had been lifted off the top of his head. "I'm okay . . . now."

Oh, man, I'm not going to cry. . . . I'm not going to cry. Yeah, right.

Two

❇

*J*eremiah Yellowboy tossed the ball in to Cody, who posted up near the basket. His head fake got Larry Lewis into the air. Then Cody took one step and banked in an easy shot.

Feather Trailer-Hobbs retrieved the ball and dribbled across the concrete driveway in front of the Lewis home.

"Hey, I like your new backboard," Cody told Larry.

"You never fake a shot like that!" Larry complained. "Every time I jump, you toss it back out to Jeremiah."

"I decided to try something new."

"I like it—as long as you don't use it on me." Larry stole the ball from Feather and dribbled toward the basket. She immediately snatched it back from him.

"So those guys heisted all of Mr. Levine's money?" Jeremiah asked Cody as they stood watching Larry and Feather play some impromptu one-on-one.

"I don't know if they got all his money, but the shoe box was empty and lying on the floor. I really didn't get to talk to Mr. Levine much. Mom and I drove him straight to the hospital in Cottonwood. She said we'd go back and check on him tonight."

"After the game," Larry called out. "I hear the Range Rattlers are pretty good."

"Bring your Band-Aids. There're always a few bumps and bruises when we play Toby, Alvarez, and Blimp," Jeremiah added.

"No problemo, amigos," Larry assured them. "Mom baked my lucky cream puffs today. We can't lose!"

Feather tugged down her yellow and pink tie-dyed T-shirt and sauntered over to Cody and Jeremiah. Her long, thin brown hair hung low on her back; her gray-green eyes danced. "I bet it was scary finding Mr. Levine like that."

"Yeah, well, I was most frightened when I thought that truck was going to run over me. It was crazy. You saw what my bike looked like."

"I was just wondering what would have happened if we had all been riding down Cemetery Creek side by side, like we did the other day," she offered.

"Someone would have gotten run over. I guess those guys were in a hurry to get away from the scene of the crime."

"That really makes me mad." Feather crossed her thin arms as she continued. "Mr. Levine moved way down there just to have some peace and quiet. It's like trouble was searching for him."

"Yeah, but at least he's not dead," Larry tried to encourage them.

"Thanks to Cody," Feather added.

"Oh, I don't know if I did much. I just happened to be the first one who came along."

"You know what else is scary about it?" Feather pressed but didn't wait for anyone to answer. "If they go to that remote place to commit a crime, they'll go anywhere. I was thinking it could happen . . . you know, in other remote areas."

"Like at a certain tepee in the woods?" Cody asked.

"Yeah. I used to think it was a great adventure to live in a tepee. Now I'm not so sure."

"What are you worried about? You've got your own room at Cody's house now," Jeremiah reminded her.

"Eh, hem! Are we going to complete our practice or not?" Larry interrupted.

Turning to brown-skinned Jeremiah, Feather lost her usual smile. "Mom's coming back on Saturday."

"She's not going to stay up in Dixie after all?" Jeremiah questioned.

"That's the thing. I don't know what she's decided. She said we'd discuss it when she got here. I don't know if I'm going to move to Dixie, back out to the tepee, stay with the Clarks, or something else."

"I think my mom likes having you at our house," Cody offered.

"Well, I'm glad someone enjoys having me around!" she sniped.

"Hey," Cody shot back, "I'm sure Dad and Denver don't mind you being around either."

Feather stuck out her tongue at Cody. "I ought to live there the rest of my life just to pester you!"

"I sure hope Mr. Levine's all right," Jeremiah interjected. "He's really a nice guy."

"I just can't believe a man would keep that much money in a box on his coffee table," Larry mused. "When I get that big NBA contract, I'm going to invest in mutual funds. That's the way to go."

"Oh, sure—advance the corporate exploitation of our remaining natural resources. I'd expect that from you," Feather lectured.

"Do what?" Larry wrinkled his face, and his blond hair flopped down into his eyes. "I just want to use money wisely."

"I have a question," Jeremiah blurted out. "If we lock away all our natural resources where we can never use them, can they still be listed as resources?"

All three stared at him with blank expressions.

"Hey . . . it was just a thought." Jeremiah shrugged.

"The philosophical Jeremiah Yellowboy," Cody grinned. "Maybe we should practice basketball. Don't count on me dribbling much tonight with these sore hands."

"Your knees don't look all that great either," Feather remarked.

Jeremiah grabbed the basketball out of Larry's hands. "Actually," he giggled, "none of Cody ever looked all that good anyway!"

"That's it, Townie," Cody threatened as he chased Jeremiah. "Like the great buffalo, your days are numbered!"

Jeremiah tossed up a wild hook shot but kept running

to keep out of Cody's grasp. "Actually, paleface, the great buffalo are making a comeback."

"Speaking of comebacks." Cody stopped to retrieve the basketball. "How's your mom?"

Jeremiah ran his hand through the black stubs of his butch haircut. "She's doing great. Really. Thanks for asking."

"It's going to seem funny not having you at the supper table tonight." Cody smiled and winked at Feather.

"Hey, didn't you hear?" Jeremiah shot back. "I'm going to keep eating with you guys. Just sort of an appetizer before I go home to eat."

Cody spent most of the practice time passing the ball quickly. Every dribble shot pain through his raw hands.

The bright blue Idaho sky filled up with puffy white clouds. The breeze was beginning to cool. They finished all twelve drills on the list Larry Bird Lewis carried in the back pocket of his Indiana Pacers shorts. They hiked through the pine-tree-covered lot to the Clark house, where Cody supplied the Gatorade as they sprawled on his front porch.

"Cody, how come you guys live in town and not out at the ranch?" Larry asked.

"Because sometimes in the winter the road out there gets closed with blowing snow. Dad always said he wanted the family safe in town. He said he could always hike in and feed the cattle, but he didn't want us isolated."

"What was it like when the sheriff interviewed you?" Jeremiah asked.

"It wasn't much. I didn't know anything. What they kept asking was what the two guys in the pickup looked like."

"What did you tell them?" Jeremiah quizzed.

"That they had sort of dark hair. That's about it."

"What do you mean, that's it?" Larry demanded.

"Well, they had ears, eyes . . . mouths . . . I don't know."

"Were they young, old, tall, short, fair, dark, blue-eyed, brown-eyed? Any noticeable scars, tattoos, or facial features?" Feather questioned.

"How would I know? I was diving for my life."

"Then one of them could have been an alien and the other one Elvis?" Jeremiah teased.

"Yeah, I guess."

"Whoa!" Jeremiah laughed. "We could sell this to the tabloids. 'Elvis and alien companion on wild crime spree in north-central Idaho. Rural lad came within inches of death at their hands!'"

"Do aliens have hands?" Larry laughed.

"Yeah," Townie howled, "but they're green and only have three webbed fingers. Always check for webbed fingers. There are aliens among us!"

"So what?" Feather announced, "My mother used to talk to aliens every Tuesday night."

All three boys turned and stared.

"What does she do, fax them?" Larry joked.

Jeremiah gulped down the last of his blue Gatorade. "Maybe she has a cellular phone that bounces the signals into space. That would be cool, wouldn't it?" He held his rather broad brown nose and spoke in a nasal monotone: "Hello, Mr. Clark. This is Ms. Optura from MTT, Mars Telephone and Telegraph. How are you this evening, Mr. Clark? It is evening, isn't it? I believe there's a six-year time difference. I hope I'm not disturbing your meal. The reason I'm calling is that I wanted to let you know that you could be saving over twelve dollars a month if you signed up with MTT to be your interplanetary phone company. And if you sign up by tonight, I'm authorized to give one free ten-minute call to anywhere in the galaxy."

Larry and Cody doubled up with laughter. "If E.T. had had this service, it would have been a short feature instead of a full-length movie!" Larry blurted out.

The tears streamed down Cody's cheeks. He tried to catch his breath. "No . . . no, really . . . Really, Feather, how does your mother communicate with the, eh, aliens?"

"You know that all three of you are jerks, don't you?"

Her gray-green eyes narrowed when she got super serious. It always made her nose look a little longer and thinner.

"Yeah," Cody admitted, "we're all jerks, but tell us how she made contact with aliens."

She crossed her freckled arms and glared at them. "At the high school cafeteria—"

"I knew it!" Jeremiah shouted. "Monsters from outer space prepare cafeteria food! I should have guessed!"

"Inside each corn dog and burrito surprise are computer chips designed to take over brain functions. By the time we've had thirteen years of cafeteria food, we turn into . . ." Larry made a weird face. ". . . adults!"

"Ahhh!" Jeremiah gagged. "And to think I always have seconds! I'm doomed! I'm doomed!"

"If I might interrupt this meeting of Morons Anonymous," Feather huffed. "What I was about to say was that my mother used to meet with about thirty aliens who wanted to become U.S. citizens at the school cafeteria every Tuesday night to teach them English as a second language. Most were Hispanic, but there were quite a few from Southeast Asia. The word *alien* doesn't have to mean someone from outer space."

"Sure . . . it's just that we assumed—," Larry fumbled.

"You assumed that since my mother communicates with nature, she must also speak to extraterrestrials. My mother is not that weird!"

"Hey," Cody shouted, then searched for how he was going to change the subject. "Do you guys want to go visit Mr. Levine with me tonight after the game?"

"Sure," Jeremiah replied. "He's a friend of my grandpa's, and I should know how he's coming along."

"Yeah, I'll go," Larry added. "How about you, Feather?"

"I assume the discussion about my mother has been concluded?" she grilled.

"Yep," Cody assured her.

"Then I'll go."

The Range Rattlers kept the Lewis and Clark Squad from making any inside baskets. Fortunately, both Jeremiah and Larry were fairly accurate from outside the arc. The score was tied eighteen to eighteen when Larry called for their last time out.

"Sorry, guys," Cody apologized, "my hands are just too sore to be any good. Feather, you better take my place for this last bucket."

Larry nodded. "All right, here's what we're going to do.

Townie, toss the ball in to Feather. Then she dribbles around at the top of the key until me and Townie get set up in the corners. Then you break to the basket, and as soon as a couple of them pull out to stop you, you pass it out to me or Townie, and we'll shoot a three. That's the only shot we've been hitting tonight."

Cody could feel the salting sweat burn his raw knees and hands. "Eh, all right, Squad," he encouraged, "just get out there and do it!"

Cody sat on the first row of the bleachers, drying the sweat off his knees with a small white towel and watched Jeremiah inbound the ball to Feather. She stayed deep behind the three-point line and dribbled from one sideline to the other. With Larry and Jeremiah set in the corners, she sprinted toward the free-throw line.

Toby Tennup and Alvarez McSwane slid across to block the lane. She faked left, dribbled the ball behind her back, and then cut between the two startled Rattlers.

Jeremiah and Larry both waved for the ball. The two startled defenders dropped back to guard the corners. Blimp Sampson blocked Feather's progress like a rock wall on a narrow path.

She didn't throw the ball in time! They're covered now!

Feather came to a two-foot stop and faked a shot to the left. Blimp took the fake and stumbled down the baseline. Pivoting to the right, she took one big step and tossed up an underhanded lay-in. The ball came off the glass and caught the rim, circling it twice before losing momentum and dropping into the net.

"All right! We win!" Larry shouted.

"She traveled!" Blimp hollered.

"Traveled? She beat you fair and square!" Larry insisted.

Blimp grabbed the top of Larry's tie-dyed T-shirt and jerked him almost off his feet. "I say she traveled!"

Cody watched Larry's eyes. He didn't flinch. "You wouldn't know traveling if it drove up in a Greyhound bus! The head fake didn't establish a pivot foot because both stayed on the ground. Then she pivoted off the right and jumped with the left. If you're going to play the game, you might as well learn the rules. Grabbing an opponent in a threatening manner is a technical, but I'll overlook it this time."

Blimp just kept staring at Larry. Then suddenly he released the T-shirt and walked away.

A flood of relief rolled across Larry's face as the three on the court rushed over to where Cody stood near the bleachers.

"Great shot, Feather!" Cody slapped her palm in a high five and then immediately grimaced in pain.

"Sorry!" she apologized.

"I thought you were going to pass it off to me or Townie," Larry grumbled.

"So did everyone on the Rattlers." She grinned.

They walked together out of the gym into the graveled Halt High School parking lot. It was now cloudy, threatening to rain. Lightning streaked behind the mountains toward the river, but there wasn't any thunder.

"Hey, let's go to the Treat and Eat for a Coke," Jeremiah suggested.

Cody shook his head. "After the way Feather embarrassed us last week, I'm never going back."

"Tish." She shrugged. "He's a little too sensitive, don't you think?"

"I, for one, am glad she spoke up," Larry declared. "If Feather hadn't said something, we'd never have figured out the riddle in that old rifle nor gotten to meet Lanni DeLira—who happened to leave me her address and made me promise to write to her every week."

"She did have an awesome smile," Jeremiah admitted. "Maybe one of the two or three best in the United States."

"The United States?" Larry gasped. "How about the universe?"

Feather circled her neck with the fingers from both hands. "Gag! Gag!"

"Well, let's at least go down to the Buy Rite Market and get something to drink," Jeremiah insisted.

"You want to race?" Larry called out.

"One, two, three—go!" Cody yelled.

Larry sprinted across the gravel toward First Street.

The other three just stood and laughed. By the time Larry hit the pavement, he glanced back. He came to a basketball-shoe screeching halt in the middle of the street.

"Very funny!" he yelled back. "I win by default."

"Winner buys the Cokes," Jeremiah announced.

"What?"

"Just joking."

Cody caught up with Larry and threw his arm around his shoulder. "Say, Larry, my main man, did I ever tell you how Halt, Idaho, got its name?"

"I've heard several different, conflicting explanations," Larry replied. "Which one is true?"

"They all are!" Cody laughed.

The two benches in front of the Buy Rite Market had at one time been green. Now they were mostly just a faded gray wood kept polished by Levis, Wranglers, Lees, and occasional Dockers.

"Here's the way the game works," Jeremiah explained. "Everyone picks a number between one and ten. Then we watch the cars that drive by the market. If I pick number four, for instance, the fourth car to pass the market is mine. If Cody picks seven, then the seventh is his. The one with the coolest rig wins!"

"Coolest rig?" Feather wrinkled her nose. "Who decides which is the coolest?"

"Hey, that's obvious. See that white Oldsmobile? It's not nearly as cool as that Dodge pickup," Jeremiah explained.

"Says who?" she questioned.

"Tell her, Cody."

He took a swig from his Mountain Dew. "Townie's right. The truck wins. Everybody knows that. I mean, which would you rather drive around town in?"

Feather stretched out her long legs in front of her. "That all depends. Suppose Brad Pitt is driving the Oldsmobile and . . . Dawson Little is driving the pickup."

"Who's Dawson Little?" Cody asked.

"A jerk I knew in Oregon."

"Can you imagine Brad Pitt driving an Oldsmobile sedan? Get real!" Larry scoffed.

"The point is, the car doesn't matter. It's who you're with that matters!" she insisted.

"You must be kidding!" Jeremiah groaned. "The rig doesn't matter? What planet are you from?"

"Haven't you heard—'Men are from Mars; women are from Venus'? A fantasy game about cars is obviously a boy thing."

"I get three," Larry announced.

"Seven," Cody put in.

"You're always seven," Jeremiah complained.

"And you're always four."

"What number are you, Townie?" Larry asked.

"Eh, I'm four. Are you in or not?" he asked Feather.

"You've got to be kidding. I'm going to buy a banana."

"A banana?" Cody asked.

"They're very healthy and full of potassium," she asserted.

The boys had finished their fourth game of Cool Rig when Feather joined them with a banana in her hand. A woman in camouflage shorts and shirt followed her out with a cart of brown paper sacks stuffed with groceries.

Feather plopped down on the bench next to Cody and began to peel the banana. "You see that woman loading all those groceries into the back of that old black Isuzu pickup?"

"Yeah, what about her? You've got some shorts just like those. Right?"

"Well, yeah, but there's something weird about her."

"Besides the smell?" Cody asked.

"You caught the drift?"

"Oh, yeah, like someone who hasn't been in a bathtub in a few weeks."

"Is that what that is?" Feather wrinkled her nose and frowned.

"Yeah."

She held the banana peel out in front of her. "I wonder if they have a can just for compost material."

"No, but there's a trash can next to the pay phone." Cody pointed.

She took one step to the trash can and then whirled around. "Cody, you know when I'm living out at the tepee, I don't get a bath too often. Did I ever smell like that woman? I'll die if you say yes."

"No, no, you never smelled like that!" he responded.

Close, but not quite that bad. Lord, I can't hurt Feather's feelings.

"Good!" she sighed. When she returned and flopped back down by Cody, she ate the banana and watched the woman in the little pickup drive away.

"Her odor wasn't the only thing strange about her."

"Oh?"

"She bought $167 worth of groceries."

"That's not unusual if you have a big family and don't get to town too often."

"No, the unusual thing was that she paid for it with 167 one-dollar bills."

"She paid for it with ones?"

"Yeah, I had to wait until she counted out every bill!"

"Maybe she's a waitress and has been saving her tip money," Cody suggested.

"If she smells like that, she can't possibly get much tip money. Where would a person come up with all ones? Maybe they were counterfeit."

"It would be a lot less work to counterfeit twenties, fifties, or hundreds."

"Seven!" Jeremiah shouted. "Cody gets Mr. Wellington's combine!"

"Hey, that's his new one! I win!"

"What?" Larry gasped. "You beat my Trans Am?"

"The Trans Am was a four-door with a dent in the right front fender."

"I didn't see any dent!" Larry complained.

"It's the McMilans' Trans Am, and it has a dent, doesn't it, Townie?"

"Yep. Mrs. McMilan ran into Mr. McMilan's snowmobile on purpose."

"Besides, the combine has a CD player, four speakers, and air conditioning!" Cody informed them.

"Oh, well, okay. Cody wins," Larry conceded.

Feather looked at Jeremiah, then at Larry, then at Cody. "This has got to be the stupidest game ever invented!"

"Obviously," Jeremiah grinned, "she's never played Deaf, Mute, and Paralyzed."

Three

●

I was only trying to be helpful."

"Well, it was a dumb idea," Cody whispered as he and Feather huddled in the backseat of the Clarks' Suburban.

"I just figured it might get kind of . . . boring for Denver to house-sit Mr. Levine's cabin all by himself," she explained. "You'd think by the way everyone reacted that I'd suggested something illegal."

"Forget it. Everyone's just a little edgy because of what happened to Mr. Levine."

"Do you think your mom will kick me out of the house now?"

"What? Because of what you said? Come on, everybody blurts out things they shouldn't."

"Everyone except your mom. She does everything perfectly."

"She's pretty incredible, all right," Cody agreed.

"And pretty. Your mom is pretty—in a mature kind of way."

She's pretty in any way! "Oh," Cody replied softly, "I guess I never really noticed."

Mrs. Clark drove to the Yellowboys' light green wood-frame one-story house and picked up Jeremiah and Larry. They piled into the middle bucket seats of the custom GMC Suburban and swiveled around to face Feather and Cody.

"Hey, I just found out my brothers are in Colorado fighting that big Antelope Creek forest fire. Did you see it on television?" Jeremiah reported.

"Eh, no. We barely had time to grab a sandwich," Cody admitted.

"Well, this fire jumped the road and is now threatening some cabins at Antelope Creek. Two Ponies and Sweetwater left to fight it last Friday."

"Are you worried about them?" Feather asked.

"They know what they're doing," Jeremiah assured her.

"You didn't answer my question. Are you worried about them?"

"My mother is kind of anxious over it."

"Yellowboy," Feather lectured, "are you going to answer me or keep beating around the bush?"

"Keep beating, I guess." Jeremiah shrugged. "Hey, speaking of beating. You guys want to go with me to a pow-wow next weekend?"

"What does that have to do with beating?" Larry questioned.

Jeremiah waved his hands up and down. "Beating drums."

"Are you going to dance?" Cody asked.

"Yeah. Grandpa's taking me to Browning, Montana.

We'll be gone all weekend. It's over the Fourth of July, so it's a big deal. It's fun, really. We can bring sleeping bags and sleep in his tepee. It's awesome—you know, just for a weekend."

"Some of us like living in tepees all the time!" Feather huffed.

"Oh, yeah . . . well, you can come, too," Jeremiah offered. "Grandpa said you'd be company for my cousin Honey. She lives over in Yakima now, but she used to live in Halt."

"Honey's going to be there?" Cody blurted out. "I'm going for sure."

"Whoa!" Larry laughed. "I haven't seen Cody that excited since he had reruns of the National Finals Rodeo on ESPN."

"I am not excited. Just surprised. I haven't seen her since first grade."

"Old flames never die," Feather teased.

"What are you talking about? This conversation is getting really stupid!" Cody huffed. "Let's change the subject."

"We've got a Thursday game and a Tuesday game," Larry put in. "We wouldn't miss any games, would we?"

"Nah, we'll be home late Monday," Jeremiah informed him.

"Will we be able to have basketball practice during the pow-wow?" Larry asked.

"Practice? Man, they have three-on-three tournaments right there at the pow-wow."

"You're kidding," Larry shouted. "All right. We can enter as a team. . . . Eh, can non-Indians compete?"

"Oh, yeah, you guys are in. Of course, it is Indian basketball."

"What do you mean, Indian basketball?" Larry asked.

"You'll see." Jeremiah grinned.

"I'll need to get a haircut before next weekend," Cody announced.

"Still thinking about Honey?" Feather asked.

"What? I was talking about a haircut!" Cody insisted.

"Were you?" she prodded.

Cody folded his arms and stared out the dark back window of the silver and black Suburban at the rolling wheat fields of north-central Idaho.

Lord, why does Feather keep pushing like that? It's not funny. I haven't seen Honey in a long, long time. It's no big thing. She's just a girl.

Well, okay, she's a cute girl.

At least she was when she was seven.

She and Feather will be together for the whole weekend! That's horrible. Feather will tell her all sorts of things about me and . . .

They'll probably all be true.

You know, Lord, it would be a whole lot simpler if we just had one relationship at a time. It gets complicated when you get to know lots of people.

"Well, are you coming with us, or are you just going to sit there and pout?"

"What? Oh," Cody stammered, "I—I wasn't pouting. I was just thinking."

"We all know who you were thinking about," Jeremiah joked.

Cody's mother left the Lewis and Clark Squad in the empty hospital waiting room while she checked to see if all of them could visit with Chad Levine at once.

Jeremiah plopped down in a large overstuffed chair. Feather examined the fruit juice machine. Cody stood by the front window and stared out at the parking lot. Larry dug through the old magazines.

"November of '94? This is a classic!" Larry waved the magazine at Cody. "This was before MJ made his comeback. Oh, man, I wonder if they have any other old magazines."

"All the magazines are old," Jeremiah laughed. "Look at this one. It has President Roosevelt on the cover."

"Which Roosevelt?" Cody teased.

"Really?" Feather stepped closer.

"I was joking!"

"Cody?" Feather flipped her long brown hair over her right shoulder. "Have you ever been in a hospital?"

"You mean, like stay in a room or just visit?"

"To stay. You know, have you ever been sick or hurt and had to stay in the hospital?"

"Nope, but I had to go the emergency room one time," he replied.

"Ahhh! Don't remind me!" Jeremiah screamed. "I was with him. It was totally gross!"

"What happened?" Larry asked.

"I just broke my arm, that's all."

Feather fiddled with the tiny gold chain that connected

the heart-shaped silver earrings in her dual-pierced ear. "How did you break your arm?"

Cody slumped down in a chair next to Jeremiah. Feather seemed to tower over them. "I got bucked off a horse. No big deal."

"Bucked off?" Larry splattered a stack of magazines back onto the table. "You mean you get bucked off, too?"

"Was it at a rodeo?" Feather asked.

"Actually . . . it was at a parade."

"A parade? You got bucked off in the middle of a parade?" Larry choked.

"Nah," Jeremiah jumped in, "the parade hadn't even started. Me and Cody were in the matched pairs competition riding a couple of Appaloosas that belong to my grandad. Well, Squat (that was his horse) started—"

"Squat!" Larry exclaimed. "The horse's name was Squat?"

"Yeah. I was riding Squint," Jeremiah added.

"Squint and Squat," Larry roared.

Shaking his head, Jeremiah turned back to Feather. "Anyway, Cody's horse got spooked and started bucking. Cody was doing pretty good until the dogs started barking. The horse went ballistic, and Cody came crashing down on a fire hydrant."

"Actually," Cody corrected, "only my left arm hit the fire hydrant."

"It was gross," Jeremiah continued. "The bone was sticking right out in the open!"

"Oh, my!" she gasped.

Larry's face turned as white as a blank piece of paper. "Larry, are you all right?" Cody asked.

Larry bent over at the waist and gulped deep breaths of air. "I'm fine. . . . I'm fine," he lied.

"Anyway, here's the funny part," Jeremiah went on.

"Funny? There's something funny about breaking your arm?" Feather probed.

"You tell them, Cody," Jeremiah insisted.

"See, the first entry in the Halt Fourth of July Parade is always our ambulance. It creeps along with sirens blaring. Well, when they got me on a stretcher, they pushed me into the ambulance and—"

"I got to ride with him," Jeremiah interrupted.

"Anyway, I was in the ambulance, and the ambulance was going to pull out of the parade and get me to this hospital in Cottonwood. But the crowd was thick, and the side roads blocked, so they had to drive me right down Main Street—right down the parade route."

"And," Jeremiah laughed, "everyone thought the parade was beginning. They all waved and waved."

"Did your arm heal up all right?" Feather asked.

"Oh, yeah. They did a good job on it." He held out his arm for examination.

Feather stared out the window away from the boys. "I spent thirty-four days in the hospital one time."

"You did?" Cody gasped. "What for?"

"Oh, it wasn't me. I spent thirty-four days sitting in a chair with my mother waiting for my brother to get better."

"Your brother!" Larry exclaimed. "I didn't know you had a brother."

"How come you never told us you have a brother?" Cody asked. "You told us you are an only child."

"I am."

"But—," Cody began.

"He died."

"Oh, man, that's . . . that's . . . ," Jeremiah stammered.

"It was nine years ago."

A tear spilled out of the corner of her eye, but she didn't try to wipe it away.

"Hey, you don't have to talk about it if you don't want to."

"It's okay."

"I thought you said your parents don't believe in doctors," Cody said.

"They don't . . . now."

"What happened?" Larry quizzed.

"We were living in this little cabin in Alaska—"

"Alaska!" Jeremiah pressed.

"I told you guys that I've lived all over. Anyway, I was about four, and my brother Larch was almost two. Our place was fairly remote, and we had to hike four miles to our car and then drive an hour to town."

Larry whistled. "That was remote, all right."

"Well, Larch—he was named after a tamarack tree— had been sick, so Mom took him to a doctor. Dad was out in the Bering Sea protesting the whaling. Anyway, the doctor said Larch had pneumonia, but since we didn't have any money for the hospital, he gave us some medicine and sent us all home."

"And it wasn't pneumonia?" Cody asked.

"Larch got worse, and a few weeks later we hiked back out and took him to the hospital. Mom pitched a fit until they admitted him. That's when they discovered what he really had."

"What was that?"

"Meningococcal meningitis. A very advanced case."

"How long did he . . . live after that?" Larry inquired.

"Just thirty-four days," she replied. "He lost his hands and then his feet . . . and then he just gave up and died. He was only two."

A tear slipped down Cody's cheek. He didn't dare let Jeremiah or Larry see his face.

"If they had caught it sooner, could they have saved his life?" asked Larry.

"The doctors said it wouldn't have made much difference, but my mother is convinced they blew it. That's why we don't go to doctors anymore."

Cody rubbed his eyes on the back of his hand. "I guess doctors aren't perfect. Sometimes they miss."

"I wish they had missed on someone besides my brother."

"I'm really sorry, Feather."

"I've never talked about it before. I don't know why I am now."

"Hey," Jeremiah tried to hide his sniffles, "that's what friends are for, Feather girl."

She turned around and looked at Jeremiah, Larry, and Cody. "You know what? I like it when you guys call me Feather girl."

"You do?" Cody quizzed.

"Yeah. It reminds me that I'm one of the gang . . . and uniquely different—all at the same time."

"Different?" Larry probed.

"You know . . . a girl!"

"Oh, yeah. That kind of different," he mumbled.

Cody's mother stepped back into the waiting room. "Mr. Levine would like a visit by all of you now. He's in room 24. I'll stay here. There isn't much space in there."

Room 24 had a heavy polished oak door that was open about a foot. The place smelled like cleaning solvent. Cody could hear his boots slam against the tile floor. He gripped the cold, polished brass door handle and pushed the door open. A white curtain hanging from a track in the ceiling kept him from seeing who was in bed.

"Mr. Levine? It's me, Cody Clark—and the others."

It was a soft, yet firm voice that replied, "Come in. Come in!"

Cody led the others around the curtain. With his unbandaged head propped up on a couple of pillows and a crisp white sheet pulled up to his neck, Chad Levine gazed at them through tired dark eyes. "I'm sorry I can't offer you any strawberries today. You will have to promise to come see me at the ranch. We'll sit on the porch and eat strawberries and cream."

"That would be great!" Jeremiah blurted out.

"How long do you have to be in the hospital?" Cody asked.

"Just tonight, I hope. I am fine actually—other than a lump on the back of my head. I owe you a major debt, young Mr. Clark."

"Oh, no, sir. I didn't do much. I just showed up."

"The sheriff said you were the one that brought me around and helped your mother get me to the hospital."

"I was just . . . coming down to bring you news about some mail," Cody explained.

Mr. Levine nodded. "Well, the Lord Almighty was good to me."

"Good to you?" Feather questioned. "You got clobbered and robbed."

"It could have been much worse. Sometimes I go several weeks without seeing anyone. It was divine providence that sent Cody down to the river."

"I thought it was his mother," Feather countered.

"Young lady, never, ever underestimate how many times the Lord Almighty uses mothers to accomplish His will. In fact, they just might be His chief instrument."

"Really?"

Mr. Levine nodded his head and then rubbed the stubble of his gray beard. "I hear your brother and a friend are going to stay at the cabin tonight."

"What friend?" Feather pressed. "It's not that Becky, is it?"

Cody glanced over at her. "Not hardly!"

Mr. Levine smiled. "Mrs. Clark said that Denver and Brett Hostlinger already drove out there."

"Oh, that friend," Feather mumbled.

Chad Levine struggled up on one elbow. "Mr. Clark, could you hand me that glass of water?"

"Yes, sir."

Wiping his mouth on the back of his hand, Mr. Levine

lay back down. "The sheriff also said that your presence on Cemetery Creek Road probably kept them from coming back."

"Coming back?"

"Yes. He figured once they looked at the take, they might have come back for more."

"You mean, they didn't steal all your money?" Jeremiah quizzed.

Levine pulled his right hand out from under the covers and waved his forefinger at them. "I will tell you something not many people know. I don't know why I'm telling you, but I am old, and you are young, and this is not a secret I want to die with me."

"What?" they echoed in unison, scooting a little closer to his bed.

"They did not steal very much money," he whispered.

"Not very much? A shoe box full of $100 bills isn't very much?" Jeremiah asked.

"Ah hah, you saw my bait."

"Bait?" Larry said.

"It was filled with 225 one-dollar bills."

"Ones?" Jeremiah choked.

"But we saw $100 bills," Cody insisted.

"You only saw one $100 bill on top. The rest were ones, but our eyes and our greed combine to think that they are all $100."

"So you lost $225 in ones and the one $100 bill?" Larry asked.

"No, the $100 bill was counterfeit. Years ago it was passed off to me in the pawn shop. I wrote in ink across the bottom 'counterfeit.' No one can spend it. I convinced the Treasury Department to allow me to keep it so I could spot the phonies better. No one anywhere could cash that bill."

"So they got $225. That's still quite a bit. Why did you call it bait?" Cody asked.

"Well, one of the things that I moved to the ranch from my pawn shop was my big safe."

"I didn't see any safe," Jeremiah replied.

"No, you didn't, young Mr. Yellowboy. It's in the basement."

"I didn't know you had a basement," Cody replied.

"That makes it doubly safe, don't you think? I keep most of my valuables down there. Of course, I keep my money in the bank. You don't think I'd leave much money just lying around, do you? I figured someone would grab the box and run out the door thinking he had robbed the old man. That way I'd get by with fairly cheap insurance. I've been there over forty years, and this is my first burglary."

Cody sighed. "It's a relief knowing you're feeling better and that you didn't lose a fortune."

"Now—" He waved them closer to his bed. "Let me tell you another secret."

All four held their breaths.

"Mutual funds!" he rasped.

"What?" Cody choked.

"Always invest in mutual funds," he repeated.

"I knew it!" Larry shouted. "What did I tell you? Didn't

I say we should invest in mutual funds?" Then he turned to Mr. Levine. "I told them that just the other day."

"Well, Mr., eh, Lewis, wasn't it?"

"Yes, sir."

"Mr. Lewis, you are a wise man. Now just how do you plan on earning the money for such a prudent investment?"

"I'm going to get a big contract in the NBA," Larry boasted.

"The NBA?"

"The National Basketball Association. I'm going to be a professional basketball player."

"Larry's a very good player," Cody explained.

"Well, he's certainly ambitious."

"That's an understatement," Feather interjected.

"And do you know what else is ambitious?" Mr. Levine continued. "Stealing 225 one-dollar bills."

"Ambitious?" Cody asked.

"Every time you go to buy something, you'd have to count out all those ones. Can you imagine paying for several bags of groceries with ones?"

"Groceries!" Feather shouted.

"Ones!" Jeremiah exclaimed.

"The lady at Buy Rite!" Larry cried.

Four

❀

*A*ren't you going out to feed Mr. Blaine's horses?" Feather asked as she shuffled into the Clark kitchen.

Cody stared at the boxes of cereal in the cupboard and finally pulled down the Cheerios. He dumped some into a deep bowl layered with frozen cherries. "Dad came back from the ranch this morning and said Eureka rolled in late last night and wouldn't need me to look after his horses for a week or so."

Feather snatched a big box of shredded wheat and stood next to the sink as she crumbled a roll into a bowl. "Kind of seems funny that Jeremiah isn't here, doesn't it?"

"Yeah. I was thinking the same thing." Cody nodded. "But I'm sure glad everything's all right with his mother."

"I thought she was going to stay at her sister's longer."

"So did I. Townie said it was just too crowded at his aunt's in Yakima."

"Is Denver coming home today, or is he staying down at Mr. Levine's?" She shuffled over to the table and plopped down in a chair across from Cody.

"He already came home."

"He did? You mean Denver's here?" Feather ran her fingers through her long brown hair and reached up to her earlobes. "I don't have on any earrings!" she moaned. "Eh, I'll be right back."

"Hey, relax. He already went out to the ranch with Dad."

"Oh, well, in that case . . ." She slumped back down and began to eat her cereal.

"Yeah, and guess what else?"

"He's decided to dump that Becky girl?"

"In your dreams. No, he said a deputy came by the cabin this morning early and reported that Mr. Levine's pickup had been found in back of the trees near Four Corners."

"I suppose that means they hopped in their rig and took off down Highway 95."

Cody spooned out a cherry pit he found floating in his cereal. "I think they came close to town and sent the lady in the camouflage shorts in to buy groceries."

"Was one of the people in Mr. Levine's pickup a woman?"

"Yesterday when they tried to run me off the road? Nah, they were both men."

"Are you sure? Sometimes people who panic make mistakes."

"I didn't panic," Cody insisted, "and I didn't make a mistake! I can tell a woman from a man."

"Well, that's good."

"What's that supposed to mean?" Cody grilled.

"Oh, nothing." Feather heaped her soup spoon with cold mashed shredded wheat and milk and then stuffed it into her mouth. "I didn't think the sheriff was all that excited when we told him about the woman who had purchased the groceries with all ones."

Cody fished out a dark burgundy cherry covered with a frosted layer of frozen milk and popped it into his mouth. "I guess we didn't have that good of a description," he mumbled.

"We told them to look for an old black Isuzu pickup. How many of those are around here?" Feather queried.

"I think it was the part about a woman who was medium height, medium build, with medium brown hair that left him a little less than excited. Besides, even if she was with the robbers, we don't know if she went north or south."

"Or," Feather added, "if they went right back into the woods."

"At least they recovered Mr. Levine's truck. Those guys didn't trash it."

Feather stared at her cereal bowl. "You know, I wish we had electricity out at the tepee. Then we could have a refrigerator, and that means we could have cold milk. I like very cold milk on my cereal."

"Good morning, you two. I'm glad you found something for breakfast."

"Good morning, Mrs. Clark," Feather replied as Cody's mother sailed into the room. The light blue ribbon tied around her hair matched perfectly her star-shaped earrings.

"I've got my bed made. And my room straightened up.

Are there any chores around the house you'd like me to do today?" Feather offered.

"Honey, you've vacuumed this house more times in the past week than it's been done in a month. The dust particles are threatening to go on strike if we get it any cleaner."

"Maybe I could, eh, wash the windows. I haven't done that in a long time. We don't have any windows, so I don't mind doing it, really."

Cody just rolled his eyes and dove back into his bowl of frozen dark, sweet cherries, Cheerios, and very cold milk. *Oh, brother. Lay it on, Feather girl.*

"You don't have to work so hard. We're delighted to have you stay with us until your mother comes back. You don't have to do chores to earn our approval. But if you want to wash windows, you may certainly do it. I'd have Cody help you, but I have another job for him."

I hope it's better than washing windows.

His mother was wearing that marines drill sergeant expression on her tanned face.

"What do you want me to do?"

"I just had a long talk with Chad Levine on the telephone. He's checking out of the hospital at 11:00 this morning. I told him we would give him a ride back to the cabin."

"Does this mean he's feeling all right?"

"Well, for a man his age, that was quite a blow. He'll need someone to help with the chores for a few days. Other than that, he's just fine."

"Who's he going to get to help him?" Cody asked.

"I volunteered you."

"Me?" Cody gulped

"What with Eureka back home, I figured you wouldn't mind a couple days of staying down in the canyon. He'll pay you ten dollars a day."

"A couple days? I'm going to stay down there? What about basketball?"

"You won't miss any games."

"What about practice?"

"You've been saying that you're getting burned out on practice anyway. I didn't think you'd mind."

"But . . . but there's nothing to do down there. It's so boring and—"

"Cody Wayne! Mr. Levine needs some help, and it's our Christian duty to help our neighbors."

"Neighbor? He's not even close to being a neighbor."

"Obviously you don't remember the lesson about the Good Samaritan," she scolded.

"I remember," Cody conceded. "Help those who need help—no matter who they are, right?"

"Right. Now Mr. Levine said you could bring a friend along with you. He'd pay both of you."

"Just one? Maybe the whole Squad could go down there, and we could—"

"Only one. Mr. Levine needs some help, not an invasion."

"Oh, I'll go with Cody. I'm used to living in the boonies," Feather volunteered.

"Your mother is due in tomorrow. I'm afraid you'll need

to stay here. Besides, Mr. Levine has only a one-room cabin—not exactly built for a young lady."

"Oh, I could get along. I live in a tepee!"

"Not with a thirteen-year-old boy, you don't."

Feather stared down at her cereal.

"I'll call Townie," Cody suggested. "He's been around animals some. We'll take our .22s, and maybe after the chores are done, we could go snake-hunting down in the rocks."

"Snake-hunting?" Feather gasped. "You mean there are snakes down there?"

"Oh, yeah. At this time of the year there will be rattlesnakes everywhere."

"Everywhere?"

"Everywhere down in the canyon. We're at too high an elevation for rattlesnakes around here."

"In that case, I think I'll just stay here and wash windows," she announced.

Cody made two quick phone calls and then wandered back into the kitchen to find his mother.

"They can't go!" he announced dejectedly. "Townie needs to stick around the house and help his mother, and Larry's family is going to Spokane."

"Well, I'm sure you'll get along fine. You've looked after stock for years."

"But what am I going to do? I'll be down there by myself. He doesn't have a TV or anything!"

"Take a book to read, a practice rope, and your .22."

"Oh, joy," he mumbled.

"And you'd better take along a more cheerful disposi-
tion."

"Yes, ma'am," he softly replied.

By noon Cody was sitting on the front porch of Chad
Levine's cabin, staring at the vast expanse of the Salmon
River Canyon.

*The chores are done, and for the next ten hours there is
absolutely nothing to do. I told Mom it would be this way.*

"Young Mr. Clark, you are a natural with livestock. I
envy you." Chad Levine spoke slowly as he rolled a large
towel-draped object out on the deck.

"You envy me?"

"When I moved down into this canyon, I knew
absolutely nothing about animals. I had to teach myself
from scratch. And, believe me, the animals and I both suf-
fered the consequences. And here you are—just a lad—and
you're so knowledgeable and at ease."

"It's nothing special. If you're raised on a ranch, it sort
of comes naturally."

"Well, I still say it's a God-given talent. Now I believe I
need to lay down for a short nap. I thought you might like
to look at this."

Mr. Levine pulled back the towel to reveal a ten-inch
diameter, three-foot-long telescope mounted on a black
cast aluminum stand.

"I can't tell you how many nights I've studied the planets and stars with this beauty." He patted the top of the
telescope. "But it also doubles as a spotting scope. I can

look over half the Joseph Plains from here. Would you like
to give it a try?"

"Yeah!"

"Well, here it is. Just use the little top-mounted scope
to line it up. Then peek through this eyepiece. You'll probably be able to spot lots of deer and elk."

"No kidding?"

"Go for it. I'm headed for a nap."

Mr. Levine scooted back into the cabin and left Cody
staring at the huge telescope.

*Okay, Lord, maybe I was wrong. Maybe there will be
some things for me to do.*

For the first fifteen minutes Cody tinkered with the
scoping telescope. He looked at the Seven Devils
Mountains, which still showed snow, examined the Joseph
Plains on the far side of the river, which were beginning to
turn brown, and finally tilted the telescope toward the
Salmon River a couple hundred feet below the cabin and
was rewarded with a close-up of three rafts full of tourists
running the rapids.

*This is almost like being in heaven and looking down
at the world. I hope there's a moon out tonight and no
clouds. Whoa! This is going to be totally awesome. But it
would be more fun if Townie and Larry and Feather were
here. Maybe Mom can drive us down sometime. I don't think
Mr. Levine would mind some company.*

Ignoring the telescope for a moment, Cody stared
across the river. *Maybe I'll go plink some rocks with my .22
now and then use the telescope after it gets dark.* He
cupped his hands over his eyes. *Is that a fire over there?*

He studied a small column that looked like smoke far out on the Plains. Cody grabbed the telescope and hurriedly focused it in on the column.

"A dirt devil?" he mumbled out loud. "No . . . it's some kind of rig! Someone's driving out there."

Wow, without this telescope I thought it was a fire. This would be a pretty good place for a fire lookout.

Looking through the eyepiece, he followed the column of dust. *I think they're headed north, which could lead them to Cemetery Creek Road . . . unless they turn off someplace. This is cool. I can't see the car, but I can watch the dust from the car.*

All right! They didn't take the turnoff toward the old Joseph Cemetery. They're still headed this way. They're on the zigzags, but when they get down to Rice Creek, they could go south. 'Course it's a dead-end that way. Unless you're my dad who won't take 'dead-end' for an answer. They might take the Center Creek Road to Canfield and Whitebird, but . . .

Cody stood up and rubbed his eyes. Then he took a deep breath and sighed.

Get a life, Clark. There's got to be more to do around here than watch dust from an unseen rig.

Cody left the giant telescope on the front porch, grabbed up his Winchester 1906 .22 rifle, and stuffed a box of cartridges into his back pocket. Peeking into the cabin and seeing Mr. Levine still asleep, he hiked out past the barn and corrals next to the house and started working his way down the mountain toward the river. Following a cow trail around the contour of the mountain, Cody plodded along. Not finding any varmits to hunt, he began to pick out rocks and granite outcroppings for targets.

They've got us surrounded, Tap! We'll have to shoot our way out. . . . What's that? They winged you in the right arm? No problem, partner, follow me. I'll have you back to Miss Pepper in no time. . . . There's one. . . . Got him! . . . Another to the right! . . . Got him! . . . And there's El Malo Hombre himself. Ping . . . whoops, I missed. Not to worry—his gun jammed. Ping. Got him! Come on, Tap, let's break for the horses. You can thank me later. You'd have done the same thing for me, partner.

Cody hiked on down the mountain with the pump .22 draped across his shoulder.

Yeah, sure, me and Tap Andrews. So what if he's a fictional character living 115 years ago? I just know we would have been friends.

Reaching a narrow rocky drive, Cody turned downhill and began to hike over toward the lower end of Cemetery Creek Road.

Lord, how come some other era than the one we live in always seems more exciting? I never wanted to live in the fifties, except maybe to watch Casey Tibbs ride Neck Tie, but I sure would like to live back in the 1870s and 80s . . . at least for a week or two. Cody the Kid . . .

Get a life, Clark.

I wonder what it's like living this isolated all the time. I think I'd get a little dingy.

A chill shock raised the hair on the back of his neck, and he froze in place at the sound of the rattles.

Where is he, Lord? I don't see him. Oh, man, he sounds big!

Cody pumped a shell into the chamber and held the small rifle to his shoulder. The sound seem to come from in front of him, so he backed up slowly and crawled to the top of a boulder about the size of a wheelbarrow.

I still can't see him! Maybe I should just try to creep back up the mountain. . . . I've got to get one clean shot at him.

There was movement in the rocks about twenty feet ahead of him. Cody finally caught sight of the slithering diamondback. The body of the snake looked about the size of Cody's arm, but he couldn't tell the length since only four or five inches at a time were visible.

There he is. He's going left. Come on, big boy.

Cody pointed his rifle to the right side of the boulder and waited for a menacing snake head to appear.

None did.

The snake no longer rattled.

He's decided to hole up behind that boulder. There's no way I'm going in there and flush him out. And there's no way I'm hiking down to the road. He must be five feet long!

Cody jumped off the boulder and lowered the .22 rifle. He reached down and scooped up a rock about the size of a golf ball and tossed it toward the rattlesnake's hideaway. Instantly, Cody raised the rifle to a shooting position.

Come on, get mad. Come on.

There was no sound. No movement. Nothing. Cody could feel sweat rolling down the back of his neck. Above, the heat of a summer sun seemed magnified by the clear blue skies.

Man, it's hot down here. He pulled up the shirttail of his sleeveless black T-shirt and wiped his face.

He'd be just the right size to skin and make a belt. Maybe Mr. Levine would like a little barbecued snake meat tonight.

Yeah, sure, Clark. You can't even get a shot at him.

Cody tossed another rock behind the boulder, but the snake didn't respond except to tune up his rattles in angry protest.

Good. He's mad. Maybe I'm standing too close. If he comes whipping up here, I'm headed back to the cabin pronto.

Suddenly a tiny cottontail rabbit popped out of a short silvery sage that grew on the mountain slope about even with the boulder where the snake hid.

Not a smart move, bunny. Two more hops and you'll be snake food.

"Hey!" Cody yelled, lifting the cocked .22 to his shoulder.

The little rabbit, startled by Cody's voice, instantly reversed his direction and leaped back toward the sagebrush. At the same moment the rattlesnake lunged toward the cottontail.

Cody pulled on the sun-warmed trigger of the '06. The snake flew several feet backwards and lay motionless, its belly to the sun.

The bunny sped away. Cody pumped another shell

into the chamber of the .22 and kept it pointed at the motionless snake.

That is one big snake! I can't believe I got him with one shot.

"Mr. Snake," he called out, "if you want to move, this would be a good time."

Cody reached down and plucked up the tiny .22 brass casing that had ejected to the ground. His dad's constant lecture ran through his mind: "Even if you can't reload them, you can pack them out. If God didn't put it there, don't leave it there."

Cody hiked to the south where the remnants of a barbed wire fence lay scattered in the rocks. Tangled in the wire was a loop of orange plastic baling twine. He untied it and stuffed in it his pocket. One of the old cedar fence posts lay broken beside the wire. Cody retrieved a rough splintery piece of wood two inches wide, four feet long, and an inch thick. Clutching the stick in his left hand and the rifle in his right, he hiked back toward the snake.

Using extreme caution, Cody crept up on the motionless reptile and whacked at the soft skin of its belly.

It didn't move or flinch.

Then he whacked it again.

Still no movement.

Breathing a deep sigh, he uncocked the hammer of the rifle and laid the gun on the big boulder next to the snake. Then he tied the orange bailing string to the stick and formed a slip knot with the other end. Cody retrieved the rifle and used the barrel to lift what was left of the snake's head. Still standing a couple feet away, he slid the slip knot loop over the head and then several inches down the body of the snake. When he raised the stick, the orange baling twine pulled tight, and he lifted the snake up into the air.

"Well, Mr. Snake, you're almost as tall as I am." He kept the snake dangling out in front of him like a flag bearer in a parade as he hiked down the steep mountain toward Cemetery Creek Road. About twenty feet above the road, Cody laid the snake on a rock and rested his left arm.

Wish I had a gunny sack. I could just . . .

A cloud of dust coming up the road from the river caught his attention.

That rig out on the Plains! It's coming this way. I saw it when it was twenty miles away. Cody sat down on the boulder next to the snake and waited.

Boy, this would be a lousy place to play Cool Rig. "All right, Cody has number seven!" That could take a month on this road. "Cody has number one." That's better.

The vehicle shot by, unaware of the audience of one.

Oh great, a beat-up compact pickup. 'Course, it does beat the competition. That's about the only way an Isuzu could win.

"Isuzu!" he hollered. "It must be her! The woman at the store with all the ones! Oh, man!"

Cody grabbed the rifle and the snake stick. He jogged down to Cemetery Creek Road and plunged into the cloud of dust that now blanketed the gravel roadway.

I've got to get a license number—or even the state.

Finding nothing in view but road dust, he began to jog up the road to the north toward Chad Levine's driveway. He broke through the dust and spotted the little pickup pulled over next to the abandoned hull of *The Pride of Astoria*.

"Hey!" *Why did I yell? What am I going to say anyway?*

The driver immediately slammed his or her foot on the accelerator, and, spinning gravel for fifty feet, the pickup fishtailed up the road.

I didn't get the license number or state or anything! I couldn't even tell if it was her driving. It must have been her. Why else would she take off in such a hurry?

He glanced down at the snake still dangling on the stick.

'Course, it might have had something to do with a dirty-faced kid running and screaming, carrying a rifle and a snake.

A wide grin broke across Cody's face.

I don't know who was in that rig, but I bet they'll have a story to tell!

All right, Clark, let's go skin a snake.

Cody began the hike up Mr. Levine's dirt driveway. This time the stick was carried like a rifle over his shoulder, and the snake hung behind him.

Five

❀

*W*hat do you mean, she's gone?" Cody quizzed his mother as soon as he entered the house. He tossed his black duffel bag to the floor and jabbed his straw cowboy hat on a peg next to several others.

"Feather went home with her mother, of course. You knew her mother was coming in yesterday," Mrs. Clark reminded him.

"But it, eh . . . just seems funny that I was gone down to Mr. Levine's for two days, and I come home to an empty house."

"Empty? Your father, I, and Denver make it empty?"

"You know what I mean. For over a week we had Townie and Feather both staying with us. It seems kind of quiet."

Mrs. Clark fiddled with putting on silver and black dangling earrings. "You should have seen it last night. Denver had a date with Becky, and your father and I were home alone. That's a rare event."

"Wow, I'll bet you were really bored." Cody nodded.

"Bored?" She smiled.

Cody thought he saw a blush in her tan face, but then he figured it was just her makeup.

"Cody Wayne, you go get your shower. I don't imagine you had a shower or a bath down at Mr. Levine's. I don't want you late for Sunday school."

"I really have to get back home. Mom didn't seem very happy that I wanted to come to church again. I guess she thinks you're brainwashing me," Feather announced as she swung back and forth on the tall swing at the Halt City Park.

"Am I?" Cody asked.

"Not yet. . . . But I do have a lot of questions to ask you sometime. But not today."

Larry, Jeremiah, and Cody plopped down in swings next to her.

"Let's see who can swing the highest," Larry challenged.

"That's just like a boy. I wear a dress, and you want me to swing high," Feather complained.

"Huh?" Larry shrugged.

"I'll take you on, L.B.," Jeremiah challenged.

Cody and Feather watched as the other two swung higher and higher.

"So you really saw that lady who bought the groceries with ones?" she asked.

"I saw the black Isuzu pickup. I really couldn't tell who was inside. They took off when they saw me with my gun and the snake."

"I bet they did! Do you think the guys who attacked Mr. Levine are out on the Joseph Plains?"

"If the Isuzu was the same one, if the lady was connected to the men who jumped Mr. Levine, if they are all still together. That's a lot of ifs."

"Well, I don't see any other explanation."

"Mom said maybe the crooks stopped and bought something from that lady and then took off down the highway. That would give her a bunch of ones."

"Maybe someone ought to talk to her."

"That's what the sheriff said. Only no one knows who she is or where she lives."

"She must live on the Plains," Feather suggested.

"Maybe, but it's so rugged and remote you could search for a year and not find anyone. Besides, the county line is the river. The sheriff doesn't have any authority over there."

"I won!" Larry yelled from high in the air.

"No way!" Jeremiah responded.

"Feather, who's higher?" Larry shouted. "I'm higher, right?"

Jeremiah, with shirttail flapping in the breeze, hollered back, "If I go any higher, I'll loop this thing!"

"It looks like a tie to me," she pronounced.

"A tie!" Larry groaned. "You've got to be kidding."

"Come on, Cody, you decide," Jeremiah prodded.

"Feather's right. It's a tie."

"It's because of limited equipment. In Indiana we had this swing that would go thirty feet high. Really!" Larry began to slow down.

"How big was that snake?" Jeremiah asked.

"About five feet."

"And you didn't bring him home?"

"I'm tanning him out at Mr. Levine's."

Larry flew out of his swing and tumbled into the grass, smearing a green stain across his gray pants. "Hey," he shouted, "I bet I had more hang time than Michael Jordan!"

"What do you mean, you're tanning the snake?" Feather asked.

"I skinned him, gutted him, and cleaned out the meat. Then I tacked the hide to a board and covered it with a layer of rock salt. Next time I'm down there, I'll check it out."

"What are you going to do with it?" she asked.

"I'd like to make a hat band out of it and—"

"Wait a minute. Wait a minute," Larry interrupted. "What do you mean, you cleaned out the meat?"

"It was a big snake. We couldn't eat it all, so we just froze the rest."

"You froze it?" Feather asked.

"You ate it?" Larry gulped.

"Did you bread it or just roast it over the fire?" Jeremiah quizzed.

"We roasted it. I like it best that way."

Jeremiah wiped his mouth with his hand. "Yeah, me too."

"Does Mr. Levine have a refrigerator and a freezer?" Feather twirled her long hair under her nose like a mustache.

"Yeah. In the basement."

"Wait a minute. Wait a minute!" Larry insisted. "Are

you telling me you actually ate a snake? This is a joke, right, guys?"

"What else does he have in the basement?" Jeremiah asked.

"It's big down there. It's like a museum. He has lots of things left over from his days of running the pawn shop in Halt."

"But he doesn't have any electricity. How can he have a refrigerator?" Feather demanded.

"Butane. He has a butane stove and fridge."

"No kidding." She shook her head and sighed. "You mean we could have a refrigerator at the tepee?"

"Sure, provided you put in a butane tank."

"You guys didn't really eat a snake, did you? You're just trying to string me along like all those stories about how Halt got its name, right?" Larry was trying to get someone's attention.

Cody ignored Larry and looked at Feather. "I suppose butane is environmentally hazardous and not acceptable to your folks."

"Are you poking fun at us?" she questioned.

"Actually, I'm not. I think it's cool. Your family knows what they believe in, and they stick to it. That's all right. I think my family's the same way. We know what we believe in, and we stick to it."

"You mean Jesus and all that?" she asked.

"Yeah. I know what it's like to be in a family with principles."

"But you don't know what it's like to be in *my* family," she asserted.

"Hey," Jeremiah called, holding his nose so his voice sounded high-pitched and muted, "this is chopper number four requesting permission from the tower for takeoff."

Jeremiah had twisted the chains on his swing into metal knots. Lying on his stomach in the swing, he clung to a support bar to keep himself from beginning the twirl.

"Chopper number four, this is the tower." Cody held his nose as he nasaled a reply. "Your mission, should you choose to accept it, is to fly behind enemy lines and retrieve 200 pounds of stolen snake meat."

"Aye, aye." Jeremiah grinned.

"You got your seat belt on?"

"Check."

"Is your seat back forward and your tray locked in an upright position?"

"Check."

"Did you take your air-sick pills?"

"Check."

"How would you like to pay for this?"

"Check."

"All right, chopper number four, you have permission to take off."

Jeremiah began his spin.

"Wait a minute. Wait a minute!" Larry hollered. "Time out. You're ignoring me. Did you eat snake meat or not?"

"Eh, yeah. I said that ten times," Cody insisted. "It's good. It tastes like stringy chicken."

"Yuck! Sometimes I'm glad I don't eat meat." Feather grimaced.

"You really ate the snake? Oh, crud! You're serious!" Larry exclaimed.

"Whoa! Look at Townie." Cody pointed to the spinning Jeremiah Yellowboy.

"I'm going to barf," Larry croaked.

"Hey, Townie, let's see you walk over to the slide. Come on. Go for it!"

Jeremiah staggered dizzily to the left, then to the right. He twirled around twice before falling down on his back. Looking up at the bright blue Idaho sky, he burst out laughing.

"All right," he hollered, "who's spinning that sky? Stop it right now!"

Feather and Cody joined in the laughter. They hiked over to Jeremiah, each offering a hand. They struggled to pull him to his feet. Still staggering and laughing, he tried to tuck in his teal green long-sleeved western shirt.

"You're not listening to me," Larry shouted. "I said all this talk about eating slimy snakes is going to make me puke."

"I didn't eat a slimy snake," Cody replied.

"You didn't?" Larry held his breath.

"It was moist but not slimy."

"Ahhh!" Larry cried, bending over at the waist.

"Oh, oh," Jeremiah responded. "I thought he was kidding."

"Larry," Cody stammered, "are you all right?"

His face white as a sheet, Larry stared with a glazed look at Cody. "I think I'll go home," came the weak reply.

"Oh, yuck!" Jeremiah gasped. "Flying isn't good on a full stomach. I'm going home, too."

"We're all going home," Cody decided. "Larry, I'll call you after dinner and see how you're feeling."

"Dinner? Ahhh!" Larry groaned.

Cody walked with Feather across the street to the Halt Community Church where she had left her bike by the back steps. A few people were still standing and visiting in the gravel parking lot.

"Do you want me to ride my bike—I mean, Denver's bike—with you back out to your place?" Cody blurted out.

"Why in the world would I want you to do that? Do you think I can't make it on my own?" she huffed.

"No, I just thought . . . I mean, you left when I wasn't home . . . maybe you wanted to talk or something."

"What would I want to talk to you about?" she prodded.

"Oh, never mind."

"Well, if you need to talk to me," she offered, "you are certainly welcome to ride out with me."

"Oh, no, I don't have anything to say, really. I just thought you'd want to talk . . . about moving back out to the tepee and how your dad's doing and whether your mom still wants you to move up to Dixie, and all that."

"Cody Wayne Clark, are you saying that you miss me?"

"What?"

"I've only been gone from your house one day, and you miss me already?"

"Miss you? Me miss you? Come on, I've got a whole houseful of people. I figured you might miss—"

"Oh," she exclaimed, "you think I should miss you!"

"I didn't say that."

"You were thinking that."

"I was not," he protested. "Oh . . . well, maybe I was a little, but I didn't mean it in a bad way."

"See. It was you who missed me." She beamed.

Cody took a deep breath and sighed. "What are we arguing about?"

Feather hiked up her long dress and straddled her bicycle. Cody turned away.

"Hey, it's all right," she explained. "I'm wearing my jeans shorts underneath."

"Feather, are you really going to move up to Dixie? Did your mom get mad that you deceived her about your staying with us? Will you be able to play in tomorrow night's game?"

"Why don't you go get Denver's bike and ride out to my place with me?" She fought to keep back a smile.

"Oh, so you *do* want me to ride along."

"Only if you want to."

"That's up to you," he insisted.

"I can't believe this," she shouted. "Cody Wayne Clark, go get that bike and meet me at the entrance to the lake. You're riding me home. Do you hear?"

"Yes, ma'am." He grinned.

"Are you sure you feel like shooting baskets?" Cody asked as Larry stood at the door bouncing the ball on the Clarks' cement front steps.

"Are you kidding? I was born to shoot baskets," Larry proclaimed.

"But you might get sick again."

"I'll be fine as long as you don't mention the 's' word."

"You got it." Cody bounded down the steps, and the two boys headed across the pine-tree-covered vacant lot that separated the houses.

"I guarantee I won't lose my lunch. I didn't have any."

"You couldn't eat?"

"We were having spaghetti."

"I can see how that might have been a problem."

Cody and Larry played for several minutes without saying much. Larry threw a left-handed hook shot that bounced off the front rim. He followed through and put in the rebound. "Is Feather going to be at the game tomorrow night?"

"She said she didn't know. I guess her mother's not talking much. Feather doesn't know what's going on."

"Did she get mad because Feather . . . you know . . . lied about staying at your house?"

"No. That's the strange part. She didn't say anything to Feather at all."

"Some families are different. Me or Kevin get caught lying, and we're in serious trouble. 'Course, Kevin hardly ever gets caught—the little twerp. He always squeals on me."

"I think her mother has other things on her mind. Feather said she thinks something crummy happened up at Dixie, because her mother came home talking about moving back to Oregon—just the two of them. But she won't tell Feather what's the deal with her dad. I guess her mom seems to be in one of those lay-out-in-the-forest-and-commune-with-the-trees moods."

"We won't have to go carry her back to the tepee like last time, will we?" Larry passed the ball out to Cody. He took a shot from the edge of the driveway.

Nothing but air.

"I hope not. You know, Larry, the more I hear about Feather's family, the more I understand why they act that way."

Larry grabbed the air ball and dribbled over to Cody. "You know, you've got to work on that."

"What?"

"Your three-point shots. You're horrible."

"Hey, that's why you, Townie, and Feather are on the team."

"Come on, let me show you. Watch. You shoot too flat. You're so strong you fling the ball in there like it was a hand grenade. What you want to do is float it in there like a giant egg landing on a silk pillow."

"What? Where do you learn stuff like that?"

Larry shrugged. "I made it up. But it sounds cool, huh?"

"You know what I was thinking?"

"Are you going to shoot the ball or just hold it?"

"I think you and me and Townie should ride out to Feather's and talk to her mother."

"Float it in, Clark!"

"I'm talking about tonight. We sit down in the living room—I mean in the tepee—and say, 'Mrs. Trailer-Hobbs, we would like to let you know—'"

"Get your shoulders square to the basket."

"'—we want you to know that we would like it very much if Feather could—'"

"Left foot forward a little more."

"'—complete the summer basketball season before you have to move.'"

"Now just balance it with your left hand. Don't grip it."

"'Feather is a very good friend, and we would really miss having her here.'"

"Okay, now tuck your elbow in a little."

"'We know you have to do what's best for your family, but we wanted you to know—'"

"Now push your hand right through the ball and let your fingers—"

"'—that Feather's important to us, too.'"

"Let your fingers dive right into the net behind the ball—or the big floating egg."

"Larry, have you been listening to me?" Cody demanded.

"Yeah, yeah. You want us to go out to Feather's and sweet-talk her mama into staying here for the summer. Now have you been listening to me?"

"Sure," Cody maintained.

"Prove it."

"Here goes the great floating ostrich egg into the silk pillow!" Cody launched the ball from clear across the driveway.

Nothing but net.

"All right!" Larry hollered. "I knew you could do it! What did I tell you?"

"I can't believe that!" Cody shouted. "I never make them from outside, and you know it."

Larry ran to retrieve the basketball. "Good coaching, my main man, good coaching!"

"Coaching? Floating eggs? Come on. It took superb concentration to ignore all that hokey stuff and just shoot the ball."

"Are you saying my coaching didn't help?"

"Give me the ball."

"You mean this giant floating egg?" Larry grinned.

"Yeah, yeah, the giant egg. Let me see if I can float another one up there."

A giant floating egg on a silk pillow! Get real. It was dumb luck. Even a blind hog can find one acorn. This ought to prove him wrong.

The ball rotated straight for the basket and seemed to Cody almost in slow motion.

Nothing but net.

"See?" Larry shouted. "Am I good or what? When you get that big basketball scholarship to the . . . the University of Idaho, well, you remember it was ol' L. B. who rounded out your game and made you the player you are."

"Basketball scholarship! Why on earth would I want that?"

"Ahhh!" Larry faked a gag. "Are you trying to get me to barf again?"

"Well, what do you think?" Cody trotted over to retrieve the basketball as it rolled out into the empty gravel and dirt dead-end street that ran up to their houses.

"Oh, I think with time you'll be able to make that shot in a game situation."

"No, I meant what do you think about riding out to Feather's tonight?"

"Oh, that. Eh, sure, but I don't have a bicycle, and neither do you."

"I can borrow Denver's, and you can . . . you can borrow my mom's."

"She has a mountain bike?"

"I wouldn't call it a mountain bike."

"I'll use my racing bike," Larry decided. "I don't even want to know what your mom's is like."

Cody led the trio into the woods at Feather's place and down the narrow dirt drive.

"One thing about living back here," Jeremiah hollered from somewhere behind Cody, "you wouldn't have many visitors. This is like living in a time warp. It makes Mr. Levine's seem like an uptown palace."

"Hey, look at that," Larry called out. "They have some visitors."

Cody slammed his hand brakes on and came to a dead stop. Up in the trees, next to the tepee, he spotted it—an old black Isuzu pickup.

Six

✦

Whoa!" Cody cautioned, signaling Larry and Jeremiah closer. "What's going on here?"

"That's the pickup from the store, right?" Larry pointed.

"It looks like it."

"And Feather's mom's VW bus is gone," Jeremiah added. "What are we going to do?"

Larry glanced back over his shoulder toward the gravel road. "Maybe we should just go home."

"There could be an easy explanation for this." Cody's voice sounded hesitant.

"Oh yeah? What?" Jeremiah pressed.

"Okay, maybe there isn't an easy answer." Cody kept staring at the tepee for signs of movement.

"I don't think anyone's here," Larry maintained. "Let's go."

"Come on. Maybe Feather needs us." Cody pumped his bike toward the tepee.

"Yeah, and maybe she needs the sheriff!" Larry protested.

"We came out here to see Feather. And that's what we'll do." Cody coasted past the pickup into the packed-dirt front yard. There was an old foot-crank sewing machine in the middle of the yard. Scattered boxes, garbage cans, and junk parts were scattered among the trees that surrounded the huge white canvas tepee.

"Feather?" Cody hollered. "Feather, it's us! Townie, Larry, and me. Feather?"

"I told you she wasn't at home." Larry hung back at the edge of the yard.

"Maybe she's out in the trees again," Jeremiah suggested.

Cody climbed off his bike and cupped his hands in front of his mouth. "Feather!" he yelled.

The woods echoed his voice, but the only reply was the soft whisper of the wind in the treetops and the twitter of birds in the twilight.

"Larry's right," Jeremiah said, still straddling his bike. "No one's here. Let's go home."

"But what if . . . ," Cody pondered. "What if Feather and her mother went somewhere in their rig, and . . . and the people with the Isuzu pickup snuck in here to look around and steal something?"

"Steal what?" Jeremiah surveyed the clutter in the yard.

"If that's t-true, then . . . then they're right inside the tepee listening—to every word we speak!" Larry stammered.

"There's only one way to find out," Cody trumpeted as he strolled toward the front of the tepee.

"Wait!" Larry cautioned. "Oh, man, don't . . . I think . . . this isn't—"

"Hello!" Cody called through the closed tent flap. "Is there anyone home? Hello? This is Cody Clark."

The deep muted voice rumbled up from behind his left ear. "And this is the voice of doom!"

Cody jumped straight up. The hairs on the back of his neck stood stiff. His heart skipped a beat. He whipped around to see that Jeremiah Yellowboy had sneaked up behind him and was speaking through cupped hands.

"Townie!" Cody groaned.

Jeremiah and Larry burst into laughter.

"Oh, wow!" Larry teased. "With a vertical leap like that, you'll be slam-dunking by your freshman year!"

"That wasn't funny," Cody pouted. "I thought I was going to have a heart attack."

"It was hilarious!" Jeremiah insisted.

Lord, things like that are only funny when they happen to someone else.

Cody began to lift the tent flap that served as a door to Feather's tepee.

"What are you doing?"

"Peeking inside. I think they usually tie this down when they leave, and it wasn't tied. So I want to make sure everything's all right."

"What will you do if it's not?" Jeremiah challenged.

Cody flipped the canvas back and stuck his head into the twenty-foot diameter conical tent. With the only light coming from the doorway and a round hole at the top, Cody had to wait for his eyes to adjust to the darkness.

The room smelled of musty incense and scented candles, although none were burning as he stared in. Several thick dark brown buffalo robes covered the ground, and the few pieces of furniture were cluttered with clothing, sacks of groceries, and books.

"Feather?" he called softly.

There were no sounds. No movements. And nothing disturbed. Cody stepped back and closed the tent flap.

"No one's home," he announced.

"That's what I've been saying for fifteen minutes," Larry called from the safety of his bicycle seat.

"Come on, Cody Wayne," Jeremiah instructed, "time to hit the trail."

"I've got one more place to look."

"Where?"

"That pickup. Have you guys got a pencil and paper?" he asked.

"Pencil and paper?" Jeremiah grinned. "Dream on. I haven't picked up a pencil since the last day of school."

"I do," Larry admitted.

"Why?" Jeremiah quizzed.

"Oh, I never know when I'll think of a new basketball play or something." Larry dug into his jeans back pocket and retrieved a small notebook and a tiny pencil. "What do you want it for?"

"Well, the sheriff said he needed a license plate number. So I'll get one for him."

He and Jeremiah walked over to the truck. Larry stayed on his bike.

"WGL 503, Nevada," Jeremiah reported.

"How about the VIN?" Cody asked.

"The what?" Larry called from across the yard.

"The vehicle identification number. They might have stolen plates. Can you read it through the windshield?"

"It looks a little smeared. Why don't you look?" Jeremiah motioned to Cody, who proceeded to the windshield and carefully wrote down the long string of numbers.

"How about the registration? Maybe there's a name," Jeremiah suggested.

Cody glanced around, then opened the door, and slid in. The cab smelled of heavy, sweet smoke, but he could find absolutely no trace of anything with a name on it.

"What did you learn?" Larry called over to him when he emerged from the truck.

"No registration or insurance papers, so they're driving illegally, and the person smokes a lot. It smells pretty bad in there."

Jeremiah stuck his head inside the cab and then pulled it back. "That's marijuana."

"Really?" Cody raised his dark brown, bushy eyebrows. "How can you be sure?"

"Because when my cousin got arrested for possession, it was me and my mom who went to clean up his place. It smelled just like this."

"Can we go now?" Larry pleaded.

"Yep," Cody replied. "I reckon there's nobody here."

"Great!" Larry's blond bangs fell down and almost covered his eyes.

Cody lifted his bike upright, straddled it, and pushed back toward the path that served for a narrow driveway.

"Wait a minute!" He stopped to look at Larry and Jeremiah. "What if Feather's mother . . . what if she like traded the VW for the pickup? And they really are here . . . and, well, Feather said her mother was in a lay-out-in-the-forest-and-talk-to-the-trees mood. Then they might be out in the woods after all."

"Whoa, you must have gotten more than just a whiff of that smoke in the pickup," Jeremiah accused. "Come on, Cody Wayne, that's too incredible for even Feather to come up with."

"No," Cody insisted, "I think we ought to hike up to the top of that mountain and take one peek while there's still daylight just in case."

"This is starting to get weird, Clark," Larry protested. "And I always figured you for a sensible fellow, too."

"Come on, you guys. It won't take us five minutes to hike up there."

"Are you sure we won't have to carry Feather's mother back down again?"

"Of course not. You guys said they weren't here, so there won't be anyone to carry."

"What about that cougar? Feather said there's a cougar out here."

"He won't attack three of us. A cougar's smarter than that."

"What if he's a dumb cougar?" Jeremiah protested.

"Then we'll have Larry teach him how to float a big egg into a silk pillow," Cody laughed, leaning his brother's bike against a tree.

"What's he mumbling about? I think he's really gone wacko!" Jeremiah winked at Larry.

"Are you really going up there, Clark?" Larry asked.

"Yep."

"Well, come on, Townie." Larry hopped off his bike. "We might have to carry Cody Wayne down the hill."

"Carry him? Why not just tie his feet around his neck and roll him down the hill?" Jeremiah proposed.

Larry scurried to catch up with the other two. "That'll work."

The climb up the tree-covered slope was steep and slow but not difficult. The boys reached the crest within minutes. Sitting on a fallen pine log, they stared west, away from the tepee.

"Can you see anything?" Larry asked.

"I can see pine, fir, cedar, tamarack, and aspen," Cody replied.

"No, I mean, can you see people?"

"I see a band of brave warriors coming home from a difficult battle. They are scared, but their hearts rejoice," Jeremiah intoned.

"What? You see what?" Larry demanded.

"That's what I see with my heart," Jeremiah explained. "With my eyes I see no one at all."

"Okay, is everyone satisfied? Can we go home now?" Larry pleaded.

Cody stood up, turned a circle, and gazed down the mountain in every direction. "You know what's funny? You can't see the tepee from here. Something about the way this mountain crowns, you can't see the tepee." He began to lead the others down the mountain.

"Are we really going to stay in a tepee when we go to the pow-wow?" Larry asked.

"Yep," Jeremiah replied. "'Course, if the weather's good, we'll probably want to sleep outside."

"Eh—" Larry stopped and glanced over at Jeremiah. "Are me and Cody going to be the only two white kids there?"

"Oh, no, there's always a few. You will be in the minority, of course. Might just do you palefaces good to be in the minority. But there's nothing to worry about."

"Jeremiah Yellowboy, the pride of the Nez Perce Nation, will protect us," Cody laughed.

"Protect you from what? The only real danger is the red-hot chili and Honey."

"Chili and honey?" Larry gagged.

"My cousin Honey Del Mateo. Cody's lost flame."

"She's not a flame. We were in the first grade. You can hardly spell your own name in the first grade, let alone have a girlfriend!"

"You know, Larry," Jeremiah began as the boys continued down the mountain slope, "I've known Cody for my whole life, and finally I've found his weakness. H-O-N-E-Y. I'll bet he learned how to spell that name in the first grade."

Cody stopped hiking and stared down the hill.

"Now he's trying to ignore us," Jeremiah needled.

"Does she play basketball?" Larry asked. "If Feather moves off, maybe we can get your cousin to move back to Halt and be on our team."

"Then we wouldn't get anything out of Clark. Remember how he played when Lanni was—"

"It's gone!" Cody shouted.

"What's gone?"

"Look down there. The pickup's gone!"

Jeremiah shook his head. "This is crazy!"

Larry locked his hands behind his head. "They were really down there when we were!"

"Maybe . . . or maybe they were out in the woods and came back to the truck after we started our climb," Jeremiah offered.

"Oh, sure, and just by accident they drove out of here before we see them." Cody shook his head.

"Do-do-do-do-do-do-do—you have now entered . . . the Twilight Zone," Larry bantered.

Cody trotted down the mountain, with Jeremiah and Larry following. Before they reached the bottom, they spotted the two-tone green VW bus driving up the lane.

"Feather!" Cody hollered. "She's back!"

By the time her mother brought the vehicle to a stop, the boys had it surrounded.

"What are you guys doing here?" Feather challenged even before she hopped out of the car. She wore cut-off jeans shorts and a tie-dyed T-shirt.

"Did you see that pickup?"

"What pickup?"

"The black Isuzu."

"When?"

"Just now. Coming out your driveway."

"Our driveway?"

"Yeah, it was parked here by the tepee, and when we came down the mountain, it was leaving."

"What were you boys doing out here on our property anyway?" Feather's mom challenged.

Mrs. Trailer-Hobbs always reminded Cody of someone who had spent too much time out in the sun. Her skin was tan and tightly drawn around her eyes, making the wrinkles and crevices seem more pronounced. Her black hair was always parted in the middle and hung almost to her waist, with generous streaks of gray. She was a little taller than Cody and thin like Feather.

"We came out to see you and Feather. But when we got here, there was a black Isuzu pickup parked by your house—eh, tepee. So we called out, but we couldn't rouse anyone."

Jeremiah scooted over by Cody to join the conversation. "We hiked up the hill just in case you were back there like the other time we came over."

"And," Larry paused and swallowed hard, "on our way down the mountain, someone drove off in the truck."

"They were probably hiding in the tepee!" Feather's mother hurried toward the dwelling.

"Eh . . . ma'am, I don't think they were. I'd like to apologize, Mrs. Trailer-Hobbs, but I did stick my head into the tepee just to see if anyone was there or if they had disturbed anything."

Feather's mom spun around. "You did?"

"I'm very sorry. I know it's your private property, and I shouldn't have done it. I hope you'll forgive me, but I was worried about Feather and you."

Mrs. Trailer-Hobbs continued to stare into Cody's eyes. Then she turned to Feather. "He really means it, doesn't he?"

"I told you he was that way, Mom."

Cody felt himself blush. "Eh, what way?"

"You do know what Feather calls you, don't you?"

"Mother! Don't you dare!" Feather protested.

"Eh . . . no, I guess I don't."

"Mother, please!"

"She calls you Mr. Nice."

"Really?"

Feather crossed her arms and gritted her teeth. "So what?"

"Why don't you boys come in and help us check to see if they took anything? I don't at all mind that you checked up on us. I'm glad Feather has some friends who care about her." Mrs. Trailer-Hobbs stepped into the tepee and glanced around the musty darkness. "A lot of people go their whole life without anyone who really gives a squat."

Lord, I—eh, I wish Mom was here. I don't know how to talk to someone else's mother.

"Maybe this is what they were after!" Mrs. Trailer-Hobbs pointed to a wooden box. Cody and the others scooted over to where she stood.

"Your medicines?" Feather questioned.

"Several are spilled or broken open."

Cody glanced at the various jars, crocks, and powder-filled paper sacks. "But . . . how would they know what to steal? They aren't labeled or anything."

"They wouldn't, but I can tell you what they were looking for. Feather, did you notice which sack they scattered?"

"The Draino?"

"Someone broke into your place to steal drain cleaner?" Larry asked.

"But you don't even have drains," Jeremiah pointed out.

Mrs. Trailer-Hobbs smiled at Feather. "That's just Feather's name for it. It's really a blend of two different Chinese roots. It produces an extremely effective laxative, but it's hard to get in the States because it looks and even tastes a little like cocaine."

"You mean they thought they were stealing drugs?"

"That would be my guess. Here's the first lesson every person should learn. If you don't know what it is, don't put it in your mouth. But as soon as they take some of that, they'll learn. Within ninety seconds it starts to take effect."

"Ninety seconds?" Larry gasped.

"Yeah. It really cleans you out. That's why I call it Mom's Draino," Feather replied.

"And that's probably where the person was when you guys rode up." Her mother nodded.

"Where?"

"In the outhouse. You didn't look there, did you?"

"No, ma'am." Cody glanced back at Jeremiah and Larry, who were both trying not to burst out laughing. "Listen, Mrs. Trailer-Hobbs, I have the license number and VIN on that pickup. When I get back to the house, I'll call the sheriff and give him the numbers."

"Why?"

"Well, they broke into your place."

"I didn't exactly have it locked."

"They took your medicine."

"Yes, and they'll pay the devil if they take it. I don't want any deputies coming out here and confiscating my medicines."

"Why would they do that?" Cody asked.

"Because some of them haven't exactly been approved by the FDA, if you know what I mean."

"Oh . . . yeah. Well, I won't mention your place, but I am going to call the sheriff with the numbers. I think that's the rig that was over on the Joseph Plains and at Buy Rite the other day."

"Well, they must have taken the old stage road south, because we drove out from town and didn't pass anyone," Mrs. Trailer-Hobbs reported.

"And if they turned left at the Forest Saloon, they would eventually get to Cemetery Creek Road without ever having to go through town or drive on the paved highway," Cody added.

"What I can't figure out is how in the world a stranger found you back here and why they thought you had drugs," Cody puzzled.

Mrs. Trailer-Hobbs glanced around the room and finally looked back at Cody. "That's a question you should ask Feather's father."

There was an awkward silence for a moment.

"Dad has lots of . . . strange friends," Feather finally offered. "They've been known to show up at our place and take things."

"The people with the black Isuzu might know your dad?" Jeremiah ventured.

"Dad was over at Mr. Levine's this spring, too. Sometimes when he gets . . ." Feather took a big, deep breath. "When he gets stoned, he talks too much."

"Now." Mrs. Trailer-Hobbs cleared her throat. "Just what did you boys want to talk to me and Feather about?"

"I don't know how to say this, so I'll just blurt it out," Cody began. "We really, really want Feather to be on our basketball team all summer, and if there's any way you could stay at least until September, we would appreciate it." Cody gulped for air. "There. I said it."

"Well . . . Mr. Nice . . . you win."

"I do?"

"Feather and I haven't exactly had a lot of good things happen to us in the last few years. You three boys— patronizing, chauvinistic, and sexist as you are—just might be the best real friends we've had for a while. So . . . we're going to stay right here until it gets too cold or until her father comes to his senses."

I don't think I want to know what that means.

"For sure we aren't moving to Oregon?" Feather asked.

"For sure," her mother replied, slipping an arm around her daughter's shoulder. "At least for now."

Feather's smile was so wide it seemed to be hanging from her earlobes, next to the bright pink dangling earrings.

The bike ride back to town went quickly. The boys saw no one on the old stage road until they came to Expedition

Lake. Cody waved to Jeremiah and Larry as each peeled off toward their houses.

He put Denver's bike inside the garage and burst through the back door. His mother and father sat at the kitchen table drinking coffee.

"Hey, listen to this. That black pickup was out at Feather's, but they didn't steal anything. Feather and her mother aren't going to move until at least October. There's some kind of trouble with her dad, but I don't know what it is. And I've got the license number of that Isuzu."

"Nevada, WGL 503?" Cody's dad queried.

"What? How did you know that?"

"The sheriff just called to report that a pickup with that plate number just tumbled off Eagle Point into the rocks by the river breaks. He wants you to come down and identify the remains."

"Remains of what?" Cody gasped.

"The truck. Apparently there was no one in it."

Seven

❖

*T*his is getting really weird!" Larry commented as he laced up his newest pair of basketball shoes. "Someone just hopped out of the pickup and pushed it over the cliff?"

Cody dribbled the ball slowly next to the bleachers just as Jeremiah strolled up wearing baggy black shorts and his tie-dyed T-shirt. He tried stealing the ball from Cody and then jumped into the conversation. "Hey, you talking about the pickup? Here's what I can't understand. The truck was stolen, right?"

"Sheriff said it was swiped two weeks ago in Winnemucca, Nevada." Cody nodded.

"So someone's afraid that they've been spotted. Let's say they know you wrote down the license number and all that, so they want to ditch the rig."

"A 200-foot canyon is not exactly a ditch." Larry finished tying his shoes and started jumping up and down on his toes.

"But the point is, wouldn't it be best just to drive it out into the forest and abandon it? It might be months before it was reported. Exploding it in a canyon just draws attention to it. That's dumb," Jeremiah reasoned.

"Maybe they are dumb," Cody suggested.

"Or maybe really smart. Maybe it's all staged to throw us off the trail," Larry added.

Cody glanced over at the blond-headed Larry Lewis. "What trail?"

"Ah hah! It's working."

Feather jogged up, wearing sandals and carrying her basketball shoes over her shoulder. Her long brown hair was braided into two pigtails.

"You guys will never in a million, zillion years guess where me and Mom had supper." She fairly glowed.

"Well, we know it wasn't at Vernalene's." Jeremiah nudged Cody. "Because you wouldn't be smiling."

"It was in Lewiston," she hinted.

Cody propped his right leg up on the bleachers and began to stretch. "How about Forrestiere's Healthy Byte Cafe and Computers?"

"We eat there all the time," Feather replied. "I said you wouldn't guess this place in a million years."

"Okay," Cody teased, "you went to McDonald's and had a Big Mac."

Feather's mouth dropped open. "Yeah . . . how'd you know?"

"No way," Larry blurted out. "You and your mom eat meat? Never!"

"Prepared by one of the world's largest multinational corporations," Jeremiah gasped. "Oh, sure."

"No, really. Mom said it was about time we found out

what all the fuss was about. It was the first time I ever ate at McDonald's."

"You're kiddin' me! There actually was a person on the face of the earth that had never eaten at McDonald's?" Larry questioned.

"Not anymore," Cody laughed. "Well, what did you think, Feather girl? Was it good?"

"I thought the meat was a little dry, but next time I'll put more ketchup on it."

"Next time?" Cody pressed.

"Yeah, like Bob Dylan said, 'The times, they are a changin'.'"

"Who's Bob Dylan?" Larry asked.

"Eh, never mind. You guys wouldn't understand anyway." Feather stole the ball from Larry and dribbled around in a circle. "I wasn't at practice, so what's the game plan tonight against the Timberline Tigers?"

"I scouted them last week," Larry began. "All they can do is shoot the three-pointers. We'll guard them tight on the perimeter, and we should be all right. Inside, they were pathetic."

"That guy doesn't look pathetic." Feather pointed out on the court where the Tigers were warming up. "He must be six-foot-two or better."

"Who's that?" Jeremiah asked.

"He's not on the Tigers!" Larry replied. "I watched them just the other night."

Cody watched the tall, dark-headed boy practice jump shots. "He's wearing a Tiger T-shirt."

"I'll go check with my dad and see what's going on."

Larry trotted toward the other end of the gym where Mr. Lewis, clipboard in hand, was giving instructions to two other teams.

Larry returned within moments, shaking his head. "I can't believe it! Terry Gitmore had an accident on his four-wheeler yesterday and broke his arm. So the Tigers were down to just two players. Then this kid—his name is Nathan Seeker—showed up tonight saying he'd just moved to town and wanted to play ball. So Dad put him on the Tigers."

"He looks good," Feather observed.

"Yeah, but can he play basketball?" Jeremiah joked.

"That's what I meant, you jerk!"

"Well," Larry said with a shrug, "we'll just have to see how good he really is."

The Lewis and Clark Squad called a time out when the score was sixteen to six.

They were losing.

When Larry, Jeremiah, and Cody reached the bench, Feather pulled the braids out of her hair.

"I can't do a thing with good, old Nathan," Cody admitted. "I can't outjump him, and even when I have position on him, he doesn't miss. If you guys have any ideas, let me know."

"Let me guard him," Feather suggested.

"I don't know," Larry mumbled. "If Cody can't slow him down, I don't think—"

"We know how he plays against a boy. But we don't know how he plays against a girl."

"Nah, we've got to—," Larry began,

"Hey," Cody blurted out, "let's give it a try. It can't get any worse. Why don't you double-team him, too, Larry. If you have to leave someone open, leave Soda McGrew. He hasn't made two shots all summer."

"I don't see how this is going help," Larry protested.

"Let's find out," Cody encouraged. "Now go get 'em!"

Cody watched as Feather trotted in and took her position next to Nathan Seeker. He could tell she was talking to him but couldn't hear the conversation. Larry took the inbound toss from Jeremiah and drove past Soda McGrew. Nathan left his position and filled the lane to stop Larry, who immediately passed off to Feather under the basket. Instead of leaping up to block the shot as he had when Cody was playing, Nathan threw his hands straight up, but backed away from Feather, who tossed in a lay-in.

There was a big smile on her face as she visited again with Nate Seeker.

What's she talking to him about? It's almost like they know each other. I wonder why she pulled her braids out? Of course, she does look older without braids.

The Tigers brought the ball in and passed it back and forth at the top of the key. Feather broke around in front of Nathan and tripped over his size-thirteen basketball shoes just as McGrew passed the ball in. Nathan Seeker reached out to keep Feather from falling. The ball bounced out of bounds untouched.

Cody marveled from the sidelines. *She did that on purpose!*

The turnover gave the ball to the Squad. Larry drove

in toward the basket. Again Nate came out to stop him, and again came a bounced pass to Feather. She faked a shot. Nathan leaped toward her this time, but she bounced it out to Jeremiah, who had been left standing at the top of the key. Seeker lost his footing and frantically tried to keep from crashing down on Feather.

Jeremiah Yellowboy's three-point shot hit nothing but net.

Feather tumbled to the floor. She reached out her hand for Nathan to help her up.

Again they were talking, and all Cody could hear was Nate's repeated apology.

Feather girl, you definitely should be an actress.

She carried on a continuing conversation with Seeker. Her voice was low, but there was a wide, easy smile.

When the score reached seventeen to eighteen, it was the Tigers who called time out.

"Feather girl, have you got him wrapped around your finger yet?" Cody asked when they huddled around him.

She lifted her head up so that her nose was slightly raised. "I don't have any idea what you're talking about!"

"Whatever you're doing, it's working. We can't let them get a good shot," Larry instructed. "I'll double-team Nate if they get it in to him. Townie, you keep Billy Fred from shooting. And let's see if we can get a lucky bounce."

"Do we have any plans for after the game?" Feather asked. "Are we going to Buy Rite and play delightfully mature games like Cool Rig or what?"

"Eh, I don't know. Why?" Cody asked.

"Nate asked me if I wanted to go to the Treat and Eat for a milk shake."

"You call him Nate?" Cody gasped. "You told him no, didn't you?"

"Why should I?"

"Because you're on our team!" Jeremiah joined in the protest.

"In case you juveniles didn't know it, going for a shake is not a team sport!"

"Are you really going?" Cody called out as Feather jogged back out on the court.

"No, but I had you worried, didn't I?" Her giggle started deep in the throat and also shone from her eyes.

Feather said something to Nathan Seeker. Both started to laugh just as the ball came in to him. Larry ran over to double-team him, and, still laughing, Seeker fired a hot pass out to Soda McGrew. Finding himself unguarded for the first time all night, Soda tossed up an awkward shot that slammed off the glass backboard, crashed into the front of the rim, bounced straight up in the air, then bounced twice more on the rim, and finally collapsed into the net.

"All right!" Soda shouted. "That's the first one of those I've made all summer!"

The Squad didn't talk much until they were all perched on the bench out in front of the Buy Rite Market.

"Hey, we gave it a good run," Cody said.

"Twelve and two is still a good record," Jeremiah added.

"It ties us for second place," Larry announced. "But you guys are right. Considering everything, it's not too bad. I think we can beat those guys next time."

"As long as Feather doesn't run out of charms," Cody concluded.

"You didn't like me doing that, did you?"

"Why should I care?" Cody shrugged.

"You did care. You were jealous, weren't you?" Feather peered right into Cody's eyes.

He turned his head away. "Jealous? Why would I be jealous? I just didn't want you to . . . I don't think . . . Anyway, we should beat them straight up."

"What's unethical about a little psychological warfare? Part of the game is psyching out the other team, right?" she probed.

"I don't want to talk about it."

"Well, I do think Cody Wayne Clark is pouting!" she declared.

"I am not pouting!" he gruffed. "Sulking maybe—but not pouting." He couldn't keep from a slight smile. "That's why you did it, isn't it? Just to watch me sulk."

"Wouldn't you like to know?" She whipped around to Larry and Jeremiah. "I get number two," she announced.

"Number two?" Larry asked.

"We are playing Cool Rig, aren't we?"

Cody spent the next morning helping Denver and his dad restack the old hay in the barn, getting ready for the new crop. After lunch and a shower, he stretched out on the living room floor and went to sleep. He heard his mother say something about groceries, but he dozed off again.

He was startled to hear a female voice at the door shouting, "Cody Wayne, open up this door right now!"

And it wasn't his mother.

Cody struggled to his feet and felt his calves tighten, almost cramp, as he padded barefoot across the brown variegated carpet and swung open the wide white front door.

"Feather?"

"I've been out here knocking on the door for five minutes. I could see you in there."

"I guess I was asleep."

"Cody, can I come in and talk?"

"Eh . . . yeah . . . no!" His voice and mind cleared about the same time. "Let's sit out here on the front porch."

"Isn't your mom at home?"

"No, I think she went to town to get groceries, and I can't have any—"

"I know, you can't have any company in the house when there's no one else at home. I used to live here—remember?"

Cody plopped down on the old wooden porch swing. His eyes were beginning to adjust to the bright light of a clear blue July summer day. Feather wore jeans shorts and a pink short-sleeved blouse that had little hearts embroidered on the pocket flaps and the collar. She had pink feather earrings on the bottom of her earlobes. He noticed tiny pink heart-shaped earrings in the upper hole in each ear.

"Did you ride your bike in just to see me?"

"Sort of. I need to talk."

"What about?"

"I've been thinking about getting my hair cut. What do you think?" Feather questioned.

"You rode your bike three miles just to ask me about your hair?"

"I've been thinking about some changes. Maybe I won't wear those tie-dyed T-shirts anymore."

"But you always wear those!" Cody protested.

"Yeah, like I said, I've been thinking about changing. Now should I cut my hair short?"

"How short?"

Grabbing her hair with both hands, she pulled it behind her head and held it there. "What if it were like this? Would that be all right?"

"Feather girl, you can cut your hair any way you like."

"What I want to know, Clark, is which way would you like it better?"

Cody squirmed in the swing and glanced across the vacant lot toward Larry's house. "You want the truth?"

"I'm counting on it."

"Well . . . I sort of like it just like it is. I think it looks cool when it's flying along behind you when you ride your bike or you go running across the basketball court."

"Okay. I won't cut my hair if you don't want me to," she declared.

"Me? But I said you could do whatever you wanted."

"And I've decided to leave it like it is. That's one thing that won't change."

"What is all this talk about changing?" Cody asked.

"Well, see . . ." She laced her fingers together and stared at them for a minute. Then she took a deep breath. "Cody, I need someone to talk to, and I don't have anyone else. Some of this is going to sound kind of, you know . . . kind of weird to be talking about. But just listen, okay?"

"Sure."

"When my mom came back from Dixie, she started talking about changing."

"In what way?"

"She said everything is open for change—if the change looks like it's for the better. Now my mother's been exactly the same ever since I can remember, so this is pretty drastic."

"Why did she say this?"

Feather took a big, deep breath and held it. She stared out at the dead-end graveled road in front of his house. The tears began to roll down her cheeks.

"Feather? Hey, you don't have to tell me anything. I'm sorry. I didn't mean to upset you. Really. Eh, you want me to get you a Kleenex or anything?"

"Mr. Nice, would you please be quiet and let me try to say this? I've been practicing these words all the way in from my place."

"Yes, ma'am."

She put her hands on her knees and stared down at her feet. "Cody, when Mom went to Dixie, she found out that Dad's been living up there with some twenty-year-old college girl. She spent a week trying to talk to him but wasn't getting anywhere. By the time she got home, she said it was time to rethink where things were headed."

Tears now streamed down her face. Without saying anything, he trotted into the house, grabbed two Mountain Dews out of the refrigerator and a box of Kleenex from the counter, and then returned to the porch. He set the items between them.

"Hey, just in case you need something."

"Cody Clark, you are the most predictable boy I've ever met!"

"I'm sorry. I don't mean to irritate you."

"Oh, hush! You aren't irritating me, and you know it. Thanks for the Kleenex—and the drink." She wiped her cheeks, blew her nose, and then popped open the soda. Taking a big swig, she looked over at Cody.

"I'm sorry about your dad and mom, Feather. I can't even imagine how much that must hurt."

"Well—" She took a deep breath. "—Mom and I stayed up all last night talking about changes."

"You mean like eating a hamburger at McDonald's?"

"Even wilder things than that."

"Like what?"

"This morning my mom drove into Halt and got a job at Buy Rite."

"Really? No kidding?"

"She's going to be in charge of the produce section," Feather announced. "But not only that, she said that as soon as she saves the money, we're going to rent a place here in town."

Cody sat up straight and turned toward her. "You mean a real house?"

"Yeah, a house with electricity and plumbing and more than one bedroom and even a telephone."

"And doors?"

"Yeah." She grinned. "You know I like doors."

"What about the multinational corporations destroying the world?"

"She said we just have to find more effective ways to get our ideas across. She said the two of us living in a tepee in the woods was not really changing the world much."

"Hey, do you get to have a post office box?"

"She stopped by and rented one this morning. Box 444, Halt, Idaho. It's the first time in my life I've ever had a post office box."

"I'll write you a letter," he blurted out.

"You promise?"

Cody glanced over at the freckles next to her rather thin nose. "Yeah, I'll write."

"I think someone rummaging through our stuff the other day kind of freaked her out, too. Anyway, Mom said it was all right to rethink everything, so I've been thinking about, you know . . . God."

"You have?"

"Mom doesn't believe in God being someone you can know. To her, God is just some force of nature. And she always said I should wait until I'm older to decide what kind of God I believe in. But now she says I'm old enough to make up my own mind."

"Wow, that's great, Feather. So what's the first thing you're going to do?"

"This is the first thing I'm going to do."

"Coming to talk to me?"

"Yeah. You're the first person I've ever known who talks to God all the time—like He was a friend or something."

"And your mom knows you're coming to talk to me about God?" Cody questioned.

"Yeah. She just said, 'Promise me you won't go to town and elope with Mr. Nice.'"

"Elope! We're—we're only thirteen."

"She was teasing, Clark!"

"Oh, yeah . . . I knew that."

"Cody, remember when I told you about my little brother dying in the hospital?"

"Yeah."

"How come that had to happen? If God really loves me like you keep telling me, how come He let that happen?"

Oh, man, I wish my mom was home. She'd know how to answer this. Lord, what am I supposed to say?

"Feather, I don't have all the answers. But it seems to me we live in a broken world where bad things like that happen from time to time."

"If it's broken, why doesn't your God fix it?"

"The way I look at it, if He made the world perfect, then only perfect people could live in it, or it would just go back to being imperfect. So if He had a perfect world, He'd need to dump all of us imperfect people and start a new race or something. Anyway, as I figure, our sins kind of messed things up, and now we have to live with it until the Lord returns. Does that make any sense?" he asked.

"I'll have to think about it some. Cody, do you think God's mad at me for being so ratty toward Him for so long?"

"I don't think so. Ratty people are the only kind He has to work with."

"But some of us . . . are rattier than others." She still stared out at the drive.

"That might be, but it doesn't seem to matter much to Him."

"Cody, would you pray for me? I wanted to talk to God myself, but I don't know . . . We've never been introduced."

Cody dropped his head. "Lord, this is my friend Feather. She wants to talk to You, but doesn't think she knows how. So if You could make it easier for her, I'd really appreciate it. Thanks, Lord. In Jesus' name, amen."

He turned to Feather. "Now why don't you talk to Him?"

"Now?"

"Yeah."

"Out loud?"

"Yep."

"What if I mess up?"

"As long as your heart's right, it doesn't matter."

"Okay . . . here goes. But don't laugh at me."

"I won't," Cody assured her.

"Eh . . . God . . . I'm Feather. I'm with Cody. . . . Eh, are You there? See, this is the way it is. I don't know anything yet, but I'm a good reader, and, eh . . . (Are you sure He's listening, Cody?)"

"He's listening. You're doing good, Feather girl. Go on. Finish your prayer."

"Well, I just want to find out what's true, God. I'm really, really tired of pretending. . . . Eh, bye. I'll talk to you later." She glanced over at Cody, then dropped her head back down. "Oh, I forgot the amen. Eh . . . amen."

Her head bobbed back up, and she was smiling, revealing straight white teeth. "Did I do all right?"

"You did great."

Suddenly she pointed down the hill where Cody's street veered off from the old stage road. "Hey, is that Mr. Levine's pickup coming this way?"

Cody stood to his feet. "Yeah . . . and Mr. Levine's driving it!"

Eight

⬤

*F*olks, we're sure glad you all decided to come to the
National Finals Rodeo here in the celebrated Thomas and
Mack Arena in Las Vegas, Nevada. History could be made
here tonight in this next event of calf-roping. As most of you
know, this event has been dominated over the past five
years by the Clark brothers of Halt, Idaho. Prescott Clark
won back-to-back championships, and he was followed by
his brother Reno, and last year by his brother Denver. Well,
this year the Clark at the top of the world standings is
nineteen-year-old Cody Clark. All he needs to do in this
tenth go-round is rope and tie his calf in less than eight
seconds."

Wearing boots, jeans, long-sleeved western shirt, and
cowboy hat, Cody Clark stood in his backyard facing the
plastic steer head and hay-bale calf. He twirled a blue
nylon rope with a big loop over his head.

"Cody nods, and the chute flies open."

He let the loop fly toward the plastic steer head and
watched as it settled down on the practice dummy's neck.

*"Clark scampers down the rope and flanks the calf . . .
one wrap . . . two wraps . . . and a hooey. . . . He's thrown
his hands in the air. Unofficially, it looks like an incredible
7.8, but we'll have to wait and see if the calf kicks free.*

*"Young Clark mounts his buckskin quarter horse and
walks him forward. The calf kicks twice and then gives up.
The judge drops the flag. The wrap holds. The time is offi-
cial. And here, ladies and gentlemen, is the new world
champion—Cody Clark, the youngest of the famous Clark
brothers from Halt, Idaho!"*

"Hey, Cody, is Denver home yet?"

Larry's high-pitched voice rang through the trees on
the vacant lot. Cody looked up from where he was slipping
his rope off the plastic steer head. "Hi, Larry. You all
ready?"

"Yeah. When's Denver getting home?" Larry hiked
through the trees carrying his basketball. His shorts
bagged to his knees, and his University of Indiana tank top
slipped down on a very tanned shoulder.

"Mom expects him back in the next half hour." Cody
pulled off his white cotton gloves and jammed them into
the right back pocket of his Wranglers.

Larry dribbled the ball on the dirt and rocks. His blond
hair was cut short on the sides but left long on the top. It
seemed to vault with each bounce of the ball. "You taking
your rope?"

"Yeah. You taking your basketball?" Cody began to coil
the rough, stiff nylon rope through his bare fingers.

"Do birds fly? Do fish swim? Does Dennis Rodman dye

his hair? Does Michael Jordan chew his tongue? Does Bobby Knight have a temper?"

Cody felt a slightly cool breeze waft through the pines. "I'll take that for a yes."

"It's really great of Mr. Levine to invite us down to his place to look at the stars and all. My mom says not many people would invite four junior highers to sleep over." Larry grabbed the basketball and spun it on the tip end of the middle finger in his left hand.

"He probably gets pretty lonesome down there. We'll have a great time. He said he was going to deep-pit bar-becue a lamb and—"

"Do what?"

"Bury a butchered sheep in a big bed of hot coals in the ground and cook it for about twenty-four hours."

"We get to eat the whole thing?"

"I don't think we'll exactly finish it off. But it's a great way to cook meat. Mr. Levine's telescope is awesome," Cody continued. "It's as big as a cannon."

"You can really see the moon up close?" Larry held the ball at a distance in his left hand, closing his left eye and squinting with his right, as if he were peering through a telescope.

"Close?" Cody pulled off his straw cowboy hat and ran his callused right hand though his shaggy and slightly sweaty dark brown hair. "I kept thinking I'd see the American flag flying. Really, it's like you could see Neal Armstrong's footprints."

"Could you see any alien footprints? Whoa! Would that

be cool or what?" Larry continued examining the basket-ball in his hand. "Ah hah! Look, an alien!"

Cody looked closely at the ball. "That happens to be a carpenter ant."

"I see its clever disguise has succeeded in throwing you off the trail. You can't fool me, alien!" He spun the ball around and bounced it, leaving a stunned huge black ant to stagger off into the pine needles. "Is Feather riding in here on her bike, or are we going to pick her up?"

Cody pulled the coiled rope up over his right arm and let it hang from his shoulder. "She said her mom was going to Lewiston and would drop her off on the way back."

"They didn't go to McDonald's again, did they? Can you imagine that?" Larry quizzed. "I can hardly believe that Feather changed that much. How do you just decide not to be vegetarian after years of eating nothing else?"

"That's only one of the changes."

"Oh, what else is she changing?" Larry faked a jump shot at an imaginary basket.

"Well, for one thing, she decided she doesn't like tie-dyed T-shirts anymore."

"No kidding! Does this mean we can get some differ-ent uniforms?"

"I suppose so," Cody admitted.

"All right! How about red and white uniform tops. My dad can get us a good buy."

"How about red and black? That way both you and Townie will be happy."

"That's cool. I can handle that. What other changes is Feather making?"

"Well, she's suddenly interested in talking to me about God. I think she's giving Him an honest look."

"You're not going to turn her into some sort of fanatic like you, are you?"

"I'm a fanatic?"

"You know what I mean. Most people figure their religion is sort of a Sunday thing. But to good, old Cody, it's a seven-day-a-week dialog."

"Eh, well, I don't know where this is leading with Feather, but I hope she's serious about searching for the Lord."

"You want to come over to my house and shoot some baskets while we wait for Denver to get here?" Larry waved toward his concrete driveway.

"Do you want to stay over here and practice roping?" Cody teased.

"Oh, sure, I can see it now—famous NBA star and cow-roper, Larry Lewis."

"Calf-roper."

"Same thing."

"Not to the cow, it isn't."

"Are you coming over?"

"Yeah, let me put my rope up. But I'm going to leave my boots on."

Within a few minutes Jeremiah Yellowboy joined them. He had a sleeping bag strapped down with bungee cords to the back of his bike.

"Thought I might as well wait over here," he hollered, coasting into the driveway. "Hey, I talked to my grandad, and it's all set for us to go to the pow-wow at Browning next weekend."

Cody tossed up a bad hook shot. "Are they going to have calf-ropin'?"

Jeremiah dropped his bike on the thick grass and walked over to them. "Maybe. They're going to have an Indian rodeo. So I would think that means calf-roping."

Cody winked at Larry. "Good. I'm going to change my name to Yellowboy and enter."

Jeremiah trotted over to retrieve a rebound. "You might want to pull off your shirt, Clark, and get a tan before we go. As it is now, you're going to stick out like a sheep in a herd of buffalo."

"You could tell them I've been sick lately," Cody laughed.

"I don't know, Cody. Thin nose, narrow blue eyes, lanky frame, skinny lips, long neck, pathetic pale skin like you crawled out from under a rock—there isn't much hope for you," Jeremiah discouraged him.

"But what I want to know is this, doc," Larry continued the tease. "Will he live through the basketball season?"

"Oh, sure—if you can call that living."

"All right! So I'm not as handsome as the pride of the Nez Perce Nation."

"You're not even as handsome as the scourge of the Nez Perce Nation," Jeremiah laughed.

"Then why's he all excited about meeting your cousin Honey Del Mateo?" Larry asked. "Obviously she won't be interested in a vanilla-skinned hick."

"She's got poor judgment and bad eyes. Maybe he has a chance." Jeremiah continued to giggle.

"Now here comes a cool-looking rig!" Cody pointed to the graveled street. "Think I'll take number one."

"Oh, sure," Jeremiah joked, "change the rules and— hey! It's Feather and her mom!"

"In a red Tahoe?"

The sport utility vehicle zipped up the drive and came to an abrupt halt on the edge of the concrete. The electric window rolled down, and Feather's head stuck out.

"Is this cool or what?" She beamed.

The boys crowded around her. "Is it yours? Did you buy it?"

"Yep. We traded in the VW bus," she announced. "It's got power everything, four-wheel drive, and even a CD player and wrap-around speakers."

"Wow! How does it sound?" Jeremiah tried to peek inside the rig.

"I don't know." Feather shrugged. "We don't have a CD." She bounded out of the vehicle, tugging a bundle that consisted of two rolled-up wool blankets and a pillow strapped together by an old belt.

Her mother shot back out of the drive and up the old stage road at about the same time Denver pulled up. Within fifteen minutes they were bouncing through the dust of Cemetery Creek Road. Only Feather sat up front in the cab with Denver.

Most of the early evening they loafed out on Chad Levine's front porch, stuffing their faces with barbecued lamb, baked beans, dutch-oven-made sourdough bread, and finishing it off with lemonade and homemade strawberry ice cream.

Finally, Cody scraped his ice cream dish for the second time and sat back and sighed. "Mr. Levine, that was just about the best meal I've ever eaten."

"Well, I'm glad I had plenty of food. I think I forgot how much young men eat."

"I'll second Cody's motion," Jeremiah added from the big net hammock stretched across one end of the porch. "I ate enough to last until the fish come home."

"The what?" Feather asked.

"Oh," Jeremiah laughed, "my grandpa always says that. I guess in the old days they waited for the salmon to return to the Clearwater River in the fall. So when they were really full, they would say that it should last until the fish come home."

"Your grandfather is a very fine fisherman." Mr. Levine rubbed his gray beard and pushed his Panama hat to the back of his head.

"Hey, we're all going to a pow-wow with Townie's grandpa next week," Cody announced.

"Will young Mr. Yellowboy be dancing?"

"Yes, sir," Jeremiah admitted.

"That reminds me." Mr. Levine stood to his feet. "I believe I have something for you."

"For me?" Jeremiah questioned.

"Yes, if I can find it. How about you young people clearing off the food and dishes to the sink? Then young Mr. Clark can show you how that telescope works. This might take me awhile to find."

Feather stood and gathered bowls of food. "Mr. Levine, those beans were very, very good. What kind of meat did you use in there? Was it chicken or what?"

Chad Levine stopped in the doorway. "Oh, my, no. That was the rest of Cody's snake." He shuffled his way toward the stairs that led to his basement.

"What? Snake!" Larry gagged. "He's kidding, right?"

"It was really good," Feather repeated.

"No, really, guys, don't set me up like that. Don't tease me. You know I have a weak stomach. Let's don't talk about snakes. . . . Let's talk about the moon. When does it come out anyway?"

"Not until dark, L. B. But what's the big deal about eating snake? You liked it, didn't you?" Jeremiah quizzed as he and Cody helped Feather clear the dishes.

"That's not the point," Larry groaned.

"Sure it is," Cody insisted. "The meat is healthy and tasty. Who cares where it came from?"

"I do."

"You ever been around one of those big commercial egg farms? You'd never eat another Egg McMuffin if you saw how they raise those chickens," Cody insisted.

"There are snake bits right now in my stomach," Larry moaned.

"I think we'd better change the subject, or Larry will start to barf again," Feather warned.

"Well," Jeremiah said with a grin, "tell us, young Mr. Clark, how did the town of Halt, Idaho, get its name?"

Larry held up his hand. "Have I heard this story before?"

"Nope." Cody grinned. "It all begins in the summer of 1881. A prospector from Silver City, Idaho, worked his way north along the Seven Devils and across the Joseph Plains. Then he tried his luck right here on Cemetery Creek.

"Most every creek had been panned out by that late date. And he was getting discouraged by the time he reached Expedition Meadow—that's where the lake is today. Before they dammed it off for a millpond, it was called Expedition Meadow. Anyway, he got tired of drifting and decided to build a cabin right there."

"So," Larry jumped in, "he decided to call it Halt because it was where he stopped or halted his prospecting?"

"No!" Cody laughed. "They called it Halt after the prospector himself. His name was Jedediah Halt."

"Oh, brother," Larry groaned, "that's the worst story yet."

"I thought it was pretty good." Feather grinned.

"Thank you. I thought it was pretty good considering I just made it up." Cody laughed.

"Are you ever going to tell me the real reason it's called Halt?" Larry asked.

"Only when you're older and more mature," Jeremiah teased.

"Yeah, right!"

Chad Levine shuffled back out onto the porch carrying a hanger with a black dusty garment bag covering an article of clothing.

"Now before I show you what's in here, I need to do some explaining. As you all know, I ran a pawn shop in Halt as a young man during the thirties and forties. It was a very difficult time to try to put groceries on the table, and many families had to part with family heirlooms. When that happened, I tried to keep the items around long enough so that some family member might have a chance to buy them back."

Mr. Levine laid the garment bag across the redwood table and sat down on a bench. "Well, sometimes the family moved on or died off or just didn't come back for the heirloom. So I sold them because I needed to buy groceries just like everyone else. But every once in a while a treasure would be brought in that was such a nice piece I just couldn't ever sell it. Most of those I have stored in trunks down in my basement. For what reason, who can say?"

"And what's in that garment bag is one of those treasures?" Jeremiah asked.

"Yes. A Nez Perce tribal family from Nespelem, up on the Colville Reservation, was down visiting relatives and needed their car repaired in order to make it home. They desperately needed some money, and I allowed them to pawn this. I assured them I would hold it until a family member returned.

"But the next day I read in the newspaper that this same family, after repairing their car in Lewiston, were involved in a car wreck just south of Spokane. All five were killed. But I still didn't want to sell this, just in case some other family members would come looking for it."

"So you never sold it?" Cody asked.

"No. I have had it for over fifty years, but I've always felt it was just on loan. Now I believe it is time to give it back."

"What is it?" Feather asked as she twisted her long brown hair between her fingers.

Mr. Levine held up the garment bag, tugging on the zipper. "It is a ceremonial jacket, and I would like young Mr. Yellowboy to have it."

Cody and the others stared at the ornate beaded tan fringed-leather jacket. "It is buckskin with hundreds of colored beads, dentalium shells, and elk teeth. I believe it was probably made around the turn of the century. I've kept the leather soft over the years, thinking I'd like to donate it to the museum sometime. But now I realize that it is meant to be displayed on the back of a young warrior-dancer. Mr. Yellowboy, this jacket is coming home to the tribe. It now belongs to you."

"You're kidding! I can have it—for free?"

"It's yours!"

Jeremiah took a deep breath and tried to wipe the tears back from his eyes. "I, eh, I don't know what to say."

Mr. Levine put his hand on Jeremiah's shoulder. "You don't need to say a word. Your eyes have said it all. Try it on. I think it might fit you well."

"I can't believe this." Jeremiah sniffed.

"Try it on, Townie!" Cody encouraged him.

"It's beautiful!" Feather added.

Jeremiah pulled the jacket on. The sleeves hung about an inch too long.

"It is perfect." Mr. Levine nodded. "You still have some room to grow."

Jeremiah ran his fingers across the soft leather and toyed with the beads, shells, and teeth.

"This is the most beautiful jacket I have ever seen in my life! We only have these in pictures—and the cheap modern imitations."

"The elders will rejoice when they see that." Cody nodded.

"My grandfather will weep like a baby! Do you have a mirror? I want to see what it looks like."

"Come with me to the basement." Mr. Levine motioned. He and Jeremiah scooted back into the cabin, leaving the others on the porch.

"Wow, this is incredible. Do you know what this is like?" Larry sighed. "This is like Larry Bird stopping by and giving you his Celtic uniform and championship ring."

"Or having someone give you Casey Tibb's inlaid purple chaps!" Cody mused.

"Or Carry Nation's axe!" Feather added.

Both boys turned and stared at her.

"Well, you know what I mean," she maintained. "Cody, are you going to show us the telescope or not?"

He stepped into the house and rolled the huge telescope out onto the front porch.

"That's a telescope?" Larry gasped. "It's huge!"

"How does it work?" Feather huddled close to Cody.

"Well, we won't be able to look at the moon and planets until after dark, but we can set it up and look over at the Joseph Plains or up and down the Salmon River."

Feather put her eye close to the eyepiece. Then she stepped back. "Okay, Captain Clark, show us how to use this thing."

He did.

For the rest of the evening one of them had an eye glued to the telescope at all times. They studied the Seven Devils Mountains, the Plains, the river, and extreme close-ups of the goats in the corral.

It was well past 11:00 P.M. before they could really study the planets. It was midnight before the full moon was high enough for easy viewing. Mr. Levine had retired earlier. Feather was to sleep on the couch in the cabin, and the boys chose the front porch. They explored the moon's surface and renamed peaks in their own honor. They spotted a moon near Jupiter, which Larry insisted was Ganymede, but Feather called it Callisto. Jeremiah, still wearing his new jacket, was the first to discover the rings around Saturn.

The moon's light was so bright that they could see its reflection off the surging, winding Salmon River below them. Even the distant, high Joseph Plains were lit up as if a dull fluorescent light hung above them.

It was Cody who spotted the moon's reflection off a windshield down next to the bridge. And it was Cody who first spotted rafters on the river.

"Why would you run the river at night?" Jeremiah asked, pulling back from the telescope.

"Just to say you did it at night, I guess," Cody suggested. "People are always trying to make something more difficult."

"But you'd miss all the beauty of the canyon—at least, most of it," Feather pointed out.

"Hey," Larry called from his position at the telescope.

"Whoever was in that car down there has hiked out on the bridge. They're carrying something that reflects the light."

"Are the rafters there yet?" Cody asked.

"No, they haven't even run the breaks," Larry replied.

"My turn!" Feather tugged at the telescope. "Wow! I think maybe there are three of them on the bridge. It's a secret rendezvous. Probably spies."

"Spies for who?" Cody asked.

"Well, they could be spying on . . . eh, okay, they aren't spies." She pushed the telescope around to the east. "The rafters are in the breaks. Boy, I wish it was daylight. It's hard to follow them in this moonlight. I think there's just one person in each raft."

"Here, let me look again," Cody insisted. Feather stepped back, and Cody strained to follow the rafts as they darted in and out of the shadows. "Yeah, there's just a pilot, but those rafts are sitting low in the water."

"You think they're loaded down?" Jeremiah asked.

"What with?" Larry probed.

"Who knows?" Cody turned the telescope back to the bridge. "Wow, they've got guns!"

"Who?" Jeremiah asked.

"A couple of the guys on the bridge. Those reflections are coming off stainless steel gun barrels."

"Are you sure?" Larry asked.

"Yeah."

"Let me see!" Jeremiah urged as Cody stepped back.

"Those rafters are about to get ambushed!" Cody exclaimed.

"What can we do about it?" Feather asked.

"Nothing. Keep watching the bridge, Townie."

"You mean, we're just going to sit here?" Feather demanded.

"All we can do is watch and pray," Cody answered. "Maybe I was wrong. Maybe the whole thing would look different in the daylight. Maybe they have fishing rods instead of guns."

The report of a distant rifle shot echoed up the canyon.

Nine

🏀

"*A*re they going to kill them?" Feather shouted.

Cody pushed Jeremiah aside and pressed his eye to the telescope. "We've got to do something!"

"Are they shooting the rafters?" Larry cried. "Oh, man, I think I'm going to barf."

Two more gunshots rang out.

"I can't tell!" Cody answered. "There are too many shadows around the bridge. But the rafters didn't come out the other side, that's for sure."

"Call 911," Larry rambled, "call the sheriff, call the FBI, call the governor, call your dad!"

"Townie, keep an eye on things." Cody stepped back from the telescope. "There isn't any 911 because we don't have a telephone. So we've got to be the 911."

"What do we do?" Feather asked.

"Well . . . we—we identify the guys with the guns and get a make on their vehicle. Townie, can you see what kind of rig they have?"

"All I can see is that it has a windshield."

"We've got to get down there in a hurry!" Cody glanced around the room.

"Down to the bridge? No way!" Larry protested. "They have guns!"

"That rig of theirs is either going to go back up on the Plains and hide out or . . . ," Cody pondered.

"Or it will come up Cemetery Creek Road right past Mr. Levine's drive!" Feather added.

"If we get down there to the old boat, we might be able to identify the vehicle, even read a license number," Cody shouted.

"How are we going to read a speeding car license number in the dark?" Feather asked.

"Let's take the telescope," Jeremiah suggested.

"We still need to slow it down," Feather put in.

"We need one of those nail strips that the police put out on the highway," Cody observed.

"Mr. Levine has a big bucket of rusty old nails out by the corner of the barn! Remember, we spotted them when we were looking at the goats," Jeremiah hollered.

Cody snatched up his rope and started across the yard. He shouted back at the others, "I'll grab the nails and meet you down at the old boat. Townie, roll the telescope down the drive, and don't tip it over."

"Oh, man . . . oh, man, I don't . . . ," Larry stammered. "What should I do?"

"Bring your basketball," Cody yelled.

"Why?"

"I don't know, but maybe you won't be so nervous!"

"What shall I bring?" Feather called out.

"Grab a flashlight if you can find one," Cody instructed.

Lord, please help those rafters. It sure looks like they are being shot at. I really hope we saw it all wrong. And help us, Lord, just to hide out and get a license number or something. We've got to do what's right, Lord. But I don't want to do something foolish.

Cody got to the edge of the corral and grabbed the bucket of rusty nails. He was surprised to see two eyes staring at him through the corral.

"Well, Mr. Goat, did we wake you up? Hey, maybe you can help us!"

I sure hope I know what I'm doing, Lord.

Cody hopped over into the corral and tossed a loop over the goat's head. Then he led the animal out of the corral, closing the gate behind him. He hoisted the heavy bucket of nails with his left hand and led the goat with his right.

"Come on, goat, time for a little late night work."

The driveway was longer than Cody remembered, and he began to panic, thinking the vehicle might have already passed by. He tried trotting down the lane, but he had to stop and rest the arm that carried the nails.

When he got close to Cemetery Creek Road, he spotted Jeremiah and Feather by the old hulk of the steamboat.

"Have they come by yet?" he called out.

"No. What do you want us to do?" Feather asked.

Cody set the bucket of nails down with a bang. "Where's the telescope?"

"In the back of the boat," Jeremiah explained. "We figured it looked iike something that belongs there."

"Where's Larry?"

Feather pointed through the night shadows. "In the front of the boat—hiding."

"You man the telescope, Feather girl. Remember, we need the state and the number, as well as model and make."

"What are you going to do?" she asked.

"Townie and me will try to get them to slow down."

"How are we going to do that?" Jeremiah quizzed.

"The goat will help us."

"Wh-what?" Jeremiah stammered.

"Come on." Cody handed the rope to Jeremiah and then used both hands on the bucket. "You lead the goat."

In the bright moonlight he, Jeremiah, and the goat trotted out into the middle of the dirt and gravel of Cemetery Creek Road.

"What now?" Jeremiah asked.

"I say we tether the goat on the right side of the road. The car will swing to the left, and we'll spread the nails pretty thick over here."

"You think they'll swerve over here and get a flat?"

"Well, I'm hoping that at least they'll slow down enough for us to read the license plate."

"What if they run over the goat?"

"Larry will barf," Cody acknowledged. "But we've got to do something."

Cody spread the nails out in a one-foot band across the road for about eight feet. Retreating to the right side of the road, he tied the goat off to the front of the boat. Then they returned to the back of the boat where Larry and Feather huddled around the telescope.

"What if they don't come up Cemetery Creek Road?" Feather asked.

Cody shrugged. "Then I've got a lot of nails to pick up for nothing."

"What are we supposed to do?" Larry's voice was even higher than normal.

"Stay out of sight and read the number. That's all," Cody instructed. "Townie, you try to get a look at the make, model, and color. Feather and Larry will read the number, and I'll try to see how many people are in the rig."

Larry flipped on the flashlight that Feather had packed down the driveway. "Yeah, I'll use this."

"No!" Cody pushed Larry's arm back. "We can't use that. It will give away our position. We don't want them to know we're spying on them."

"Wow, did you see that?" Jeremiah hollered.

"What?" Cody demanded.

"When Larry pointed the flashlight back into the telescope, it shot a stream of light out the eyepiece so strong it bounced off the trees on the top of that butte over there," Jeremiah replied.

"Do it again, Larry!" Cody called.

Larry flipped on the light, and the beam again shot across Cemetery Creek Canyon.

"It's just a tiny beam, but it must go for miles!" Cody exclaimed. "But turn it off. We don't want them to know we're over here."

The three huddled down in the hull of the boat, waiting for sounds of a rig driving up the road.

"Mr. Levine! Why didn't we wake up Mr. Levine?" Cody sighed.

"You want me to go get him?" Feather asked.

"I, eh—," Cody stammered.

"Someone's coming!" Jeremiah shouted.

"Get in your positions!" Cody called out. "Townie, get down by the goat. Larry, you and Feather man the telescope as soon as the rig's headlights are past you."

"Where are you going?"

"To the other side of the road. I'll hide in those rocks over there. One of us is bound to read the license."

"Hey," Larry yelled as Cody sprinted across the road, "do snakes sleep at night?"

I sure hope so. Lord, this is getting more complicated. Please keep us safe.

Hiding deep in the rocks, Cody peeked out at a narrow, high-mounted headlight speeding up Cemetery Creek Road.

It's a Jeep! Only a Jeep has headlights like that. I saw a Jeep right after I found Mr. Levine unconscious! They've had a Jeep out on the Plains all this time.

When the vehicle approached the old boat, Cody heard Jeremiah shout at the goat. The goat brayed and darted toward the road, spotted the oncoming headlights, and dove back for the boat. The Jeep swerved over by Cody.

No license plate? That's illegal. They could get a ticket for that.

The Jeep rumbled over the top of the nail patch and kept going.

Cody watched the small, narrow red taillights disappear around a bend in the road. He ran across the road to the others.

"So much for the nails." He shrugged.

"And the license plate. They didn't have one," Larry reported.

"There were two men and a woman in the Jeep," Feather informed them.

"You could tell that?" Cody challenged.

"Yes, I could," she insisted.

"Larry, bring the flashlight. I've got a lot of nails to pick up. Townie, get the goat out of the road. He did a great job."

Cody had just cleaned up the roadway and rejoined the others at the old boat when they spotted a lantern and a shotgun-carrying Chad Levine scurrying down the driveway.

"Oh, wonderful!" he called. "I see you caught him."

Jeremiah glanced up at the oncoming lantern. "Caught who?"

"Truman."

"Who's Truman?"

"The goat you have roped. He will kick his way out of the corral if he senses a cougar or a coyote on the prowl. I heard him bellowing down here. Oh, my, you brought the telescope and everything. Well, I better tether him up for the night so we can all get some sleep. My word, young Mr. Clark, what are you doing with a bucket of rusty nails?"

"Eh, Mr. Levine, it's a long story. We'll fill you in on the way up to your place."

And they did.

By the time they reached Levine's yard, the old man was shaking his head.

"You really think you heard gunshots in the canyon?"

"Yes, sir. We could see the fire flash, and then in a couple seconds we heard the report. I don't know if they were warning shots or murder or what. But they seemed to be flashing toward the rafters."

"I don't know why anyone would be on the river at night. But we should check it out. I'll finish getting dressed, and we'll drive down to the river," Mr. Levine announced.

"How about those guys in the Jeep?" Larry asked.

"We'll have to drive out to a phone and report that to the sheriff," Mr. Levine added.

While he was getting ready, the others huddled on the front porch.

"I can't go down there," Larry groaned. "What if those rafters are shot up or something? You know what a weak stomach I have."

"I think maybe I should stay with Larry," Feather offered. "You know, just so he won't be alone."

"Oh, I'll be all right," Larry maintained.

"I said, I'm staying here. And that's that!" she growled.

"Well, you two turn that telescope back toward the

bridge and see if you can spot anything. Me and Townie will go with Mr. Levine."

"Be careful," Feather cautioned.

"Yeah. Maybe the whole thing was nothing."

"Oh, sure. You don't believe that for a second," she challenged.

Cody and Jeremiah piled into the front seat of Mr. Levine's old black pickup.

"This is the first time I've ever rode shotgun when I carried a shotgun," Jeremiah announced as he sat next to the passenger's window, holding the Winchester Model 12 between his legs.

"On what side of the river did you see the commotion?" Mr. Levine asked as he crouched over the steering wheel and stared out at the dimly lit gravel road.

"It was on the south side. But it's hard to tell much of anything with only moonlight," Cody tried to explain.

They reached the river and turned west for a mile before they came to the bridge. The moon was straight over the Salmon River Canyon and cast a blue glow on everything. There was a coolish breeze blowing upriver. Mr. Levine parked right in the middle of the narrow bridge with its short wooden guardrails.

"Young Mr. Clark, you carry the lantern. Mr. Yellowboy, you tote the first-aid kit, and I'll carry the shotgun," he instructed. "I don't want that gun going off by accident."

Cody could hear the roar of the river under the bridge and see the white water crash off the rocks in both directions. *I don't even know why they raft this in daylight. There's a reason the Indians called it the River of No Return.*

"Which direction from here?" Mr. Levine asked.

"Look . . . down there!" Jeremiah pointed through the night shadows. "I think the rafts are over there!"

"Boys," Mr. Levine called, "I know I'm a slow old man, but I want you to let me lead the way. I'm not sure what we'll find, and it would be best for me to be first on the scene."

"Yes, sir," Cody replied, dropping back a ways.

"Hey, I could stay up here with the truck if you want me to," Jeremiah offered.

"That might be good. We'll call you if we need help," Levine replied.

The gravel road turned abruptly to the east along the river for about a quarter of a mile before a right turn brought it back to the south and the zigzag climb out of the canyon to the Joseph Plains. But Cody and Mr. Levine didn't follow the road. Instead they began the descent through a jumble of car-sized boulders to the west of the bridge.

Cody could see both rafts but little else.

If they shot them and tossed the bodies in the river, they won't be found until they bob to the surface at Little Granite Dam on the other side of Lewiston. Lord, if we can't help them . . . I don't really want to find any bodies. The only reason I'm not up at the cabin with Larry or there at the truck with Townie is because they thought of it first.

"The rafts have been sliced up," Mr. Levine reported as he reached the dark rubber carcasses. Cody scooted closer and held the light.

"Looks like they took something. The empty waterproof cargo boxes are scattered all over," Cody reported.

"Do you see any people?"

Levine, standing on the rock like a sentinel with a shotgun, surveyed the moonlit landscape.

"No, I don't see anyone!"

Like a trumpet blast above the rumble of the timbrel drums came the shout. "Hey! Over here! We're over here!"

Mr. Levine jumped. The hair stood up on the back of Cody's neck. They strained to see where the voice was coming from.

"Where are you?" Levine shouted.

"Under the bridge," came the reply. "Hurry! My partner got shot!"

Mr. Levine and Cody scurried across the boulders and into the darkness under the bridge. Carrying the lantern, Cody spied a man in jeans, hiking boots, and black T-shirt lying across the rocks, bound hand and foot with gray duct tape.

"Boy, I'm glad you came along. I can't believe anyone came down here in the middle of the night."

"Perhaps the Lord Almighty sent us." Mr. Levine nodded. "Do you have a pocketknife, Cody?"

"Yes, sir."

"Well, cut this man loose. Give me the lantern, and I'll search for the other one."

Even in the shadows, Cody could tell that the bearded man was in his late twenties or early thirties. He had a full beard, and his hair hung down to his shoulders. Cody carefully sliced the tape on his wrists and then on his feet.

"Over here, Cody. Here's the other one!" Mr. Levine shouted.

"Is he . . . alive?"

"Shoot, yeah, I'm alive!" a voice shouted. "Alive enough to kill them that ambushed us!"

Cody and the first man reached Mr. Levine about the same time and discovered another bearded man with blood soaking through the jeans on his left leg.

"We've got to get a tourniquet on that leg," Mr. Levine decided.

The first man retrieved a nylon braided rope. "I'll tie it off with this." He cut the man loose from the gray tape as Cody held the lantern above them.

"What happened? Why did those guys in the Jeep ambush you?"

"You saw what happened?" the first man asked.

"Yeah, we were up on the side of the canyon with a telescope. We saw them blast you out of the river."

"Which direction did they go?"

"Right up Cemetery Creek Road. They were driving a white Jeep."

"We've got to catch up with them. They stole our . . . stuff!" the second one demanded.

"We'll get you up to the house and try to get ahold of the sheriff to come down and get this thing cleared up. Meanwhile, I'll run you into the hospital in Cottonwood," Mr. Levine insisted.

With his arm around his friend's neck, the wounded man struggled to climb out of the boulders. Cody still carried the lantern and Mr. Levine the shotgun.

"Is everyone all right?" Jeremiah hollered out over the bridge.

"One man's wounded, but he'll live," Cody reported. Then he turned to the wounded man. "Why did they ambush you? What did they steal?"

"Gold—they hijacked our gold!" the wounded man complained.

"You had gold?" Cody pressed as they crept up to the road.

"We've been prospecting up on California Creek. Had our gold stashed in those containers. They knew what they were after, but I don't know how."

"Why are you rafting at night? And why not put in at Riggins and drive to wherever you're going?" Cody asked.

"You don't understand. These other prospectors would swarm the place if we brought this out to Riggins. We like taking it clear to Lewiston. That way they, eh, have no idea where we found it."

"Well," Mr. Levine added, "someone knew you were going to be here."

"I'll kill 'em," the wounded man growled.

"We'll leave law enforcement to the sheriff," Mr. Levine insisted.

"No sheriff. We can handle this ourselves."

"We've got to get you to a doctor at least."

"Get me to some water so I can clean up and bandage this leg."

"Old man, we want to buy this truck from you."

"It's not for sale."

"Let me clarify this. We aim to catch up with those who

stole our . . . stuff. Either you can sell us the truck, rent it to us, or we just take it. Have you got that clear?" With lightning speed the man shoved Mr. Levine and grabbed the shotgun.

Ten

✳

*B*utch," the wounded man ordered, "you drive. Put the kids and this old man in the back with me. Drive to this guy's cabin, and I'll get my leg bandaged up."

"Every minute we delay, Sundance, they're gettin' further away," Butch warned.

"I know where they're headed, and they don't know I know. We'll catch 'em, and we'll kill 'em. Ceilia was with 'em. I saw her in the Jeep."

They know the others? Kill them? Steal the truck? Lord, this isn't . . . these aren't innocent rafters or prospectors.

"Which way, Pop?" Sundance growled.

"Up Cemetery Creek Road to the old boat. Then turn right up the driveway."

Cody, Jeremiah, and Chad Levine huddled in the back of the pickup while the one called Sundance sat at the back of the pickup bed with the shotgun pointed in their direction. The bright moonlight revealed the dust fogging up on the road behind them. It also showed the pained expression on the wounded man's face.

"Look, you take the truck. Just don't harm the boys," Mr. Levine pleaded. "You really need to get your leg taken care of. Gold surely can't be worth losing a leg over."

"Gold? Oh, it's worth its weight in gold, all right. I'll survive. It looks worse than it is."

"It's *your* life, son. But if you don't get that leg taken care of in a couple hours, you'll end up losing it. And if you don't get it looked at by noon tomorrow, you're going to lose a whole lot more than your leg."

"Shut up, old man! I could blast you and these boys to kingdom come!"

Mr. Levine shook his head. "Son, that's a shotgun. Even at this close distance, the shot will spread. Now look at your aim. You pull the trigger, and your partner will take the blast in the back of the head. And we'll plunge right off into the canyon. It's your leg. I just don't want anyone to lose their life."

The pickup took a wild turn to the right at the boat and then bounced and jarred up the driveway. The wounded man's face reflected increased pain.

Jeremiah was the first to hop out of the truck.

"Hold it right there, kid!" the man with the shotgun shouted as he tried to lift himself out of the rig. He kept the gun aimed toward Jeremiah as his partner lowered him out of the truck. "You three stay together! Now where's your sink? I need some clean towels and some scissors."

I hope Larry and Feather know enough to hide!

Butch led the way to the front door of the cabin. He was followed by Mr. Levine, Cody, and Jeremiah. The wounded gunman limped along in the rear, pointing the shotgun at the others.

"Where's the light switch?" Butch muttered.

"I don't have any electricity," Mr. Levine explained. "Cody, light a lantern for me."

"Yes, sir." Cody moved past the others and fumbled to light a kerosene lantern on a small shelf by the front door. He was relieved that in the dim flickering light of the room, neither Larry or Feather could be seen.

Lord, keep them safe and out of sight.

Now the one named Butch began to give orders. "Sundance, there's a sink over against that far wall. You can clean up there. Old man, you find him some bandages. I'll keep the gun pointed toward these two—just in case you try anything funny."

Cody glanced over at a nervous Jeremiah Yellowboy. The wounded man cut his pants leg off and groaned in pain as he tried to clean up his injured leg. Cody was glad it was too dark to see the wound.

Retrieving some towels and sheets, Mr. Levine laid them on the counter next to the sink. "I have a first-aid kit you're welcome to use," he offered.

"Get it for me!" The man was breathing hard. His voice sounded angry and uneven.

"It's out in the truck. You want me to go out there?" Mr. Levine questioned.

"Get over here!" Butch demanded. "We'll send the boy out. That way he can't drive away. You hurry back, or this old man and your dark-skinned friend will be dead, do you hear?"

"Yes, sir." Cody nodded.

"Now go on!"

Cody ran out into the yard. He was only faintly aware of a cool breeze and the stillness of the night. Opening the driver's side of the pickup, he reached across the floorboard to clutch the green canvas first-aid bag. He laid it in the seat and reached down with his hand and pumped the accelerator on the old pickup.

"What are you doing that for?"

The voice and the hand on his shoulder caused Cody to jump and bash his head into the doorjamb.

"Feather!" he moaned. "You scared me to death! Mr. Levine's truck backfires a lot if it gets too much gas."

"What's going on, Cody?"

"The other guys stole something from these guys, and these guys are going to steal the pickup and chase the others down."

"What will they do with you and Townie and Mr. Levine?"

"Tie us up or something. You and Larry keep out of sight so you can untie us. These guys are rough, and they have the shotgun. Don't take chances."

"What can I do?"

"Hide good," Cody whispered. "And pray for us."

"Pray? Me? I can't pray."

"Sure you can. You did a great job the other day. I've got to get in the house. Where's Larry?"

Feather pointed up the hill.

"What's he doing up there?"

"He took the telescope and the flashlight. Said he was

going to try pointing it up the canyon and send some Morse code."

"Really? It can't hurt. Go hide!" Cody took off running back to the cabin. As soon as he bounded through the door, Butch grabbed him by the shirt collar and almost lifted him off the ground.

"What took you so long out there?"

"I bumped my head."

"You what?"

Cody leaned his head toward the lantern and pointed to a red lump in his brown hair. "Look, I was in a hurry and crashed into the doorjamb."

"I thought I heard you talking!"

"I was calling myself some names," Cody explained.

The man released him, and he took the first-aid kit over to the wounded man who now had his bare leg fairly clean and a towel pressed against the wound. The belt tourniquet was still tight on his upper thigh. Cody thought the man looked about thirty, and he was extremely tanned on his arms and face. Digging through the bag, Sundance pulled out a bottle of iodine, gauze, and a roll of adhesive tape.

"You've got to help me, kid," he instructed.

"I don't know how to—"

"You're going to learn. When I pull back this towel, you pour that iodine right into the wound."

"How much?"

"Pour it all. Then I'll slam that gauze down on top of it. Are you ready?"

Cody was breathing fast. *Don't panic. Don't pass out, Clark. It's just like doctoring sick cows. You can do it.*

"I said, ready, kid?"

"Yes, sir."

"Okay . . . ready." The man jerked back the towel to reveal bloody, ripped flesh. "Pour!"

The second Cody poured the red liquid out of the amber bottle, the man began to scream. It was a piercing, mind-deadening scream and reminded Cody of a wounded cougar that he and Denver had once cornered in a brush corral. Instead of pulling away, Cody continued to pour the liquid. It was as if he had stood back and was looking at the whole scene on a large-screen television.

When the bottle was empty, the man slapped down the gauze on his leg and caught his breath.

"Are you all right, mister?" Cody was able to croak out.

Sundance leaned against the counter and breathed hard. "Get me that sheet."

"Yes, sir." Cody handed him the sheet, and Sundance began to wrap it around his leg over the iodine-soaked gauze.

"You need any help with that?" Cody asked.

"Why should you want to help?" the man growled.

"'Cause you're hurting and need help," Cody answered. He took the end of the sheet and began to wrap the leg.

"The tighter you pull that, the better it will be," Mr. Levine called out from the other side of the room.

Cody pulled the sheet bandage tight and began to wrap tape over it.

"I can't figure you, kid. Why are you helpin' me out?"

"Look, Mr.—eh, Sundance, I don't know what kind of

mess you're in, but I sure hope you get your leg taken care of."

With his leg bandaged, Sundance limped toward the man with the gun.

"Old man, you got another car around here?"

"No."

"Well, we're going to take your pickup. We have to get our goods back, and it seems to be the only vehicle."

"We goin' to tie them up?" Butch asked, pointing toward Cody and the others.

"Nah, they aren't going anywhere. It must be miles to the next house, and it's a cinch they can't call for help." He looked over at Cody. "You done good, kid. I'm obliged."

"You got another box of shells for this shotgun?" Butch asked Mr. Levine.

"Over there on the table."

Keeping the gun focused on Levine, Clark, and Yellowboy, Butch backed over to the table and snatched up the box of cartridges. "I want you three over here. Lay down on the floor—facedown!" the man hollered.

"Is he going to shoot us?" Jeremiah whimpered.

"Butch, don't hurt 'em," Sundance ordered.

"I'll do what needs to be done!" he snapped. "Now down on your faces!"

The blast was like a muffled explosion, and Cody thought Butch had pulled the trigger. He and Jeremiah stared at each other as they lay there.

"In the yard!" Butch yelled just as another blast sounded.

Sundance turned off the lantern, cracked open the door, and peered out into the moonlight.

"It's the pickup backfiring. Someone's trying to drive it off," Cody hollered.

"Who's out there? Can you see anything?" Butch yelled, sprinting to the doorway.

"Looks like a couple of them headed this way."

Who? Is it Larry and Feather . . . or neighbors? Who's trying to start the pickup?

He couldn't see anything in the dark room but felt Mr. Levine tap him on the shoulder and then motion for him and Jeremiah to crawl behind the couch. All three were moving toward the door to the back porch when the front door burst open. Two people stepped into the room and were met by the barrel of the shotgun crashing into their heads.

Cody heard the thud as the bodies dropped to the floor.

"Close the door," Butch yelled. "Turn on the lantern."

Peeking from behind the couch, Cody saw the flicker of a match and then the glow of the lantern.

"It's those two bushwhackers!" Sundance growled. "What are they doing back here?"

The ones in the Jeep? Maybe we did slow them down! Cody looked back and saw Mr. Levine slowly open the door to the porch.

"Where's our goods?" Sundance barked out at the unconscious men on the floor.

Butch stepped over to the window and pulled back the shade to peek out. "There's a Jeep over by the barn with two flat front tires."

"Who's in the pickup?"

"It must be Ceilia."

"This is our lucky day, Sundance." Butch pointed the shotgun at the men lying on the floor. "The goods must be in the Jeep."

Cody motioned for Mr. Levine and Jeremiah to crawl on out to the porch. *What goods? What is worth risking your life over?*

"Being shot in the leg is not a good day! But don't shoot 'em yet. If she hears gunfire, she might panic and drive off with our truck."

Butch reached down and pulled a dark windbreaker off one of the men sprawled on the floor. Then he dumped a cardboard box of magazines. Handing the shotgun to Sundance, he searched the other downed man and pulled a revolver out of a back pocket.

"What are you going to do?" Sundance asked.

"Go get that truck."

When Butch turned off the lantern, Cody sneaked out into the still night air. Not spying Mr. Levine or Jeremiah, who had gone ahead of him, he grabbed up his rope off the deck and crept around to the side of the cabin to watch the yard. Butch approached the pickup carrying the empty cardboard box in front of his face as if it were full of supplies. Suddenly the driver stepped on the gas and shot out of the yard.

Butch ran after the rig with raised gun but didn't shoot. As the pickup drew even with the barn, Cody saw a large object hurled out of the loft of the barn and into the windshield of the truck.

A basketball?

The sudden impact caused the driver to swerve to the left and ram into a metal stock tank. Water sprayed straight up in the moonlight. The driver's head slammed into the windshield. The horn of the old truck blared as the unconscious driver slumped across the steering wheel.

Butch ran across the yard toward the stalled truck. Cody stepped out of the shadows, built a quick loop, and tossed it straight at the running man. He jerked the rope tight around the man's arms and chest, causing him not only to lose his grip on the revolver but to fly off his feet and crash to the dirt. Cody had a knee on the man's back and was applying two wraps and a half-hitch to Butch's hands, using the free end of his rope, before the man caught his breath.

"What are you doing?" the man screamed.

"Larry, bring me a handful of those orange baling twines!" he yelled in the direction of the barn. "Hurry!"

Butch struggled to his feet and was tugging at the rope when Larry arrived to hand Cody the plastic twine. Even with his hands tied, Butch started to sprint back to the cabin. From out of the darkness again the big round sphere flew. This time it struck the man right on the bridge of the nose. He stumbled and fell.

One wrap, two wraps, and a hooey!

Cody threw his hands into the air when he had the man's feet tied. He looked up in time to see Sundance limp out the front door and promptly trip over something that had been stretched across the step. He fell flat on his face.

In the shadows, Cody saw Jeremiah and Mr. Levine standing above the man with a pitchfork at his neck.

Cody ran to the downed man and tied his hands with the orange plastic baling twine.

"Kid, I kept Butch from shooting you, and this is the thanks I get?"

"Mr. Sundance, you'll be in the hospital by sunup. That's the best I can do for you." He tied the man's feet as well.

"Feather, you and Larry tie up that woman in the pickup before she comes to. Jeremiah, help me tie the two in the cabin."

They had just finished and met back at the front door when headlights flashed up the Levine driveway. Mr. Levine, holding the shotgun, motioned for them to get back into the cabin.

"Maybe it's more of them!" he warned.

"No, it's the sheriff!" Cody called, running out into the yard.

"Cool! He got my signal," Larry shouted.

With gun drawn, the sheriff and a deputy bolted from the sports utility police vehicle. "What's going on, Levine? Put the shotgun down!"

The next fifteen minutes were the most hectic and confusing Cody had ever experienced. All four kids and Mr. Levine seemed to be talking at once.

When the sheriff got the full story, he sent for two more officers and radioed for Cody's dad to come pick up the

Lewis and Clark Squad. It was not until all four had said their good-byes to Mr. Levine and piled into the Clark Suburban that Cody had a chance to explain things to his mother and father.

"See, those two in the Jeep and the woman had been camping out on the Plains and coming to the river every night for a couple weeks because they knew about the shipment."

"What shipment?" his mom asked.

"Well, Butch and Sundance—"

"Who?" his dad quizzed.

"The two men in the rafts. They had grown a big crop of marijuana up in the wilderness area somewhere and were shipping it down to Lewiston to be transferred to a barge heading downriver to Portland."

"But," Feather broke in, "these bushwhackers were waiting for them. While they waited, they robbed Mr. Levine and came snooping around our tepee."

"How did they all end up at Mr. Levine's?"

"I guess the nails we threw on the road punctured their tires. They came back looking for Mr. Levine's truck, which they had stolen the other day."

"But what about those two rafters?" Cody's dad pressed. "How'd they get to the cabin?"

"We gave them a ride," Cody reported.

"That was nice of you," his mother commented.

"Well, one was hurt, and we thought they were just some rafters that had been robbed."

"The sheriff said they had over $250,000 worth of marijuana with them," Larry chimed in.

"Larry signaled the neighbors, and they were the ones that called the sheriff," Cody informed them.

"Neighbors?" Mr. Clark shook his head. "It's five miles to the Buckhorn Ranch!"

"Cool, huh?" Larry grinned. "I may patent it as the Lewis Long Range Light Transmitter."

"Feather stopped one of them with a basketball, and Townie held another down with a pitchfork."

"Cody tied them all with two wraps and a hooey," Jeremiah declared.

"It was totally awesome," Larry added. "Of course, I almost barfed about six different times."

"I had no idea the canyon could be so dangerous." Cody's mother shuddered.

"Yeah, Mr. Levine said he's thinking of moving to Halt so he can get a little peace and quiet," Cody laughed.

"You could all have gotten seriously hurt. I'm not sure you behaved in the wisest fashion," Mrs. Clark scolded.

"We weren't going to get hurt, Mrs. Clark," Feather responded. "I prayed that God would protect us. Did Cody tell you that he taught me how to pray?"

"No, I don't think he did."

"Yep. He did. You know, Cody and the Lord are pretty tight. Anyway, he showed me how, and I was praying really hard all the time."

"Well, that's good."

"I even think God spoke to me tonight," she added.

"You do?" Cody asked. "What did He say?"

"Throw the basketball," Feather confided.

"What?"

"Well, when you tied that guy's hands, and he got up and started running to the cabin, it was like I heard a voice saying, 'Throw the basketball.' Do you think that was God?"

"Either God or Larry!" Jeremiah laughed. "He always wants us to throw the ball more."

"Hey, what time is it?" Larry asked.

"A little past 3:30. It will be daylight by the time we get you guys home," Mr. Clark reported. "You've had quite a night."

"Daylight! . . . We ought to have an early practice when we get home," Larry proposed.

"At four in the morning?" Cody gasped.

"Well, it's a cinch I'm not sleepy!" Feather said.

"I won't be able to close my eyes for a week," Jeremiah added.

Cody watched as his dad glanced over at his mom. He could see her wink and nod.

"Sure, why not? I'll fix them some breakfast. When they crash, they'll sleep for two days," she predicted.

"Hey, I just thought of a new play!" Larry exclaimed. "I'm going to call it the Canyon Crunch. Huddle up, guys, huddle up! See, it starts when Townie passes the ball to me. . . . Oh, man, am I good, or am I good?"

For a list of other books by Stephen Bly
or information regarding speaking engagements
write:

Stephen Bly
Winchester, Idaho 83555